John Creasey – Mast

Born in Surrey, England in 1908 into) in which there were nine children, John Creasey grew up to be a true master story teller and international sensation. His more than 600 crime, mystery and thriller titles have now sold 80 million copies in 25 languages. These include many popular series such as *Gideon of Scotland Yard*, *The Toff*, *Dr Palfrey* and *The Baron*.

Creasy wrote under many pseudonyms, explaining that booksellers had complained he totally dominated the 'C' section in stores. They included:

> Gordon Ashe, M E Cooke, Norman Deune, Robert Caine Frazer, Patrick Gill, Michael Halliday, Charles Hogarth, Brian Hope, Colin Hughes, Kyle Hunt, Abel Mann, Peter Manton, J J Marric, Richard Martin, Rodney Mattheson, Anthony Morton and Jeremy York.

Never one to sit still, Creasey had a strong social conscience, and stood for Parliament several times, along with founding the *One Party Alliance* which promoted the idea of government by a coalition of the best minds from across the political spectrum.

He also founded the British Crime Writers' Association, which to this day celebrates outstanding crime writing. The Mystery Writers of America bestowed upon him the Edgar Award for best novel and then in 1969 the ultimate *Grand Master Award*. John Creasey's stories are as compelling today as ever.

INPECTOR WEST SERIES

Look Three Ways at Murder

John Creasey

HOUSE OF
STRATUS

This edition published in 2014 by House of Stratus, an imprint of
Stratus Books Ltd., Lisandra House, Fore Street,
Looe, Cornwall, PL13 1AD, U.K.
www.houseofstratus.com

Typeset by House of Stratus.

A catalogue record for this book is available from the British Library
and the Library of Congress.

ISBN 07551-3595-4
EAN 978-07551-3595-0

Chapter One

The First Look

For Paul Bennison, it was a normal morning.

A normal morning, for him, was very good. He was a contentedly married man, with three children – a girl aged seventeen, and sons aged twelve and eight. His wife was equally happy. They were not a particularly demonstrative couple, but had a oneness, an identity of outlook on life, which helped them to see many things in much the same way.

If a joke was funny to Paul, it was likely to amuse Isobel. If some incident seemed tragic or sad or beastly to one, it was likely to seem much the same to the other. They were not alike in taste, Paul liking the symphonies, Isobel preferring light orchestral music; Paul would bury himself in books which attempted to be serious, Isobel, when she read at all, preferred the romantic novel. In films and plays their tastes differed, too, but they shared antipathy to farce, Shaw and Anouilh.

It was a normal morning, even to the moment of waking. Paul practically always woke first. Today he was aware of the daylight, the sound of birds in the London suburban street, footsteps of the early-to-workers, the distant hum of cars. Soon he was aware of blurred vision, and realised that it was Isobel's fair, fluffy hair between him and the window. She had slept without a sleeping net, and would have to battle with her hair much more than usual this morning.

He smiled, snug in the warmth which seemed to glow from their naked bodies.

There was only one reason for Isobel dropping off to sleep without a hairnet; one reason equally precious to them both. In their eighteen years together, that essential oneness had always revealed itself in moments like last night's. No words, no preparation, until the moment of desire and decision; probably no thought until a few minutes before.

Soon, exhaustion.

Later, the kind of after-glow which curved Paul's lips and made Isobel's hair fluffy against the window. He resisted the temptation to turn round and cuddle her, lay on his back until he was fully awake, then heard the clock downstairs strike.

"... five, six, seven."

"Just about right," he murmured, and permitted himself a few more minutes of warmth and comfort, before pushing the bedclothes back carefully. There was no need to wake Isobel yet. He could wash and shave and call the kids. These nearing middle-age days, when he was uneasily conscious of his waistline and the fact that he was at least twenty pounds overweight, he had only toast and coffee for breakfast, so it didn't matter whether Isobel was up to get it or not. She would want to be up in time to cook the children's breakfast.

Dressing-gown on, he closed the door softly, and went along to Rose's room. She was asleep. But whispering came from the room shared by the two boys, black-haired Paul the Second, fair-haired Michael. Paul Bennison senior opened the door and looked in, to find Michael on his back in bed, wearing only his pyjama trousers, Paul sitting by the window, telling a story. It was difficult to be sure who enjoyed it most – the teller of the tale or the listener.

"Ten minutes, chaps," Paul said.

"Okay, Dad," That was Michael.

"Okay," Paul said.

Yes, it was a normal morning, with no sense of impending disaster ...

"You should have called me earlier," Isobel protested, sitting up when he went in with the tea. The sheet slipped from her shoulder and uncovered her breast, and at the same time Michael called: "Can I come in, Mum?"

"Get washed first," Isobel called.

"I *am* washed."

The sheet was soon safely in position.

Breakfast was normal, too. Paul ate while sitting in the window seat and looking out on to a pleasant rather narrow stretch of lawn, with a herbaceous border on one side, against the fence with the Pendletons, next door on the right. There had been very little rain this summer, but there was vivid colour from antirrhinum, aster, daisy and marigold, and the dahlias were beginning to open, although they were not likely to be big blooms this year.

As Paul ate his toast, Isobel cooked the children's breakfast, hair still a little untidy, and legs bare – which meant that she hadn't stayed long enough to pull on a belt. She could do without a belt quite well. Her figure was a little thicker but not so very different from the days when they had first met; Paul doubted whether she would ever get what she most dreaded – middle-aged spread. Yet her dieting was spasmodic. Her legs were full, with firm, strong-looking calves, tapering away to nice ankles. Her feet poked into heel-less rope slippers bought last year when they had taken the first family holiday abroad; on the Costa Brava.

Paul thought, as he had a hundred times about that holiday: And everybody told me it would be cheap!

He smiled to himself; it had been worth it.

The rush of the children to see him off as he started out for the station was normal. So was Isobel, appearing at the last moment, waving. He thought how fresh she looked this morning; it was hard to believe that she had a daughter of Rose's age.

He met the usual neighbours on the way to the station.

He caught the usual train.

It was a Friday; pay-day, the day when he would make up the salaries of the thirty-one members of the staff who were paid weekly. He would draw the usual five hundred pounds, and that would leave enough petty cash for the rest of the week. He had collected five hundred pounds on a Friday so often and without the slightest trouble, that he gave it very little thought.

Five hundred pounds, these days, wasn't a sum large enough to attract the wage snatchers; they went in for the really big money. He had only a hundred yards to walk from the office, a hundred yards crowded with people. It did not really occur to him that there was danger, although after every big wages snatch, Isobel would worry and ask him if he took the proper precautions. Kent, the ageing office manager, would fuss a little and have one man go ahead of him and one man follow, to reduce the risks to an absolute minimum.

Bennison was lucky to get a seat on the train.

The office was only fifteen minutes' walk from Waterloo Station – a brisk walk over the new Waterloo Bridge, which gave the best panoramic view of any of the London bridges, whenever he thought to look, or whenever he took visiting relatives on a quick tour.

It was a calm, slightly misty, sunny morning; not yet too warm even for August. The river was almost like glass. No craft yet stirred on it. The big office building on the south bank near the Festival Hall was almost finished – in fact some of the offices were occupied; nothing really went on for ever, not even building.

His office was on the fringe of Covent Garden. It was in a little block of old buildings, really three houses knocked into one. The company, Revel & Son, made all kinds of cartons and packing-cases, containers and wrapping. For years there had been talk of building a small factory somewhere out of London, but the Covent Garden property was freehold, and the problem of delivery very simple from here. Much of their business was in urgent, special orders – there was no real mass production in anything they did.

Paul Bennison preferred being here, and hoped that the factory would never be more than a dream in old Revel's mind.

Kent, very grey, short, thick-set, with wispy eyebrows and a continually harassed manner, was already in his office. The office staff worked on the top floor, and could overlook part of the market.

"Good morning, Paul."

"Hallo, George."

"I'm a bit worried this morning," Kent said.

"What's on your mind?" Bennison unlocked his desk, and went to the safe in the corner where all the wages books were kept. Little dockets, envelopes, everything was ready. On the outside of each envelope was the amount that had to be put inside. It also showed deductions for P.A.Y.E. tax, health insurance, voluntary deductions for charities, deductions for those who were in the company's pension scheme. The real work was always done on Thursday.

Bennison took out the wages book and the box of dockets.

"Harry Myers won't be in," Kent announced.

"We'll manage," said Bennison. "What's the matter with him?"

"His wife says he's got a bit of a temperature, and she thinks he ought to stay in bed during the week-end," replied Kent. "I know we can manage, but I don't like you going to the bank with only one escort."

Bennison looked at him, and checked a laugh; it wasn't a laughing matter for George Kent, who was an old fusspot – but as nice a chap as one could hope to find behind a managerial desk.

Bennison himself, tall, still nearly as dark as his younger son but with a few flecks of grey showing, was as distinguished-looking, even handsome, as Kent was ordinary.

"We haven't had any trouble in ten years," he remarked. "I don't see why we should start this morning. Charley can come along behind, as usual."

"I would come myself, but Mr Revel will be in sometime during the morning, and you know what he's like if I'm not here."

"You worry too much," Bennison said lightly.

He did not worry at all; he did not give a serious thought to the possibility of trouble.

Charley was the messenger and odd-job man, an old merchant seaman with a good record, in his sixties, not so physically powerful as he had once been, but alert, conscientious and absolutely loyal. As he and Bennison started to go through the offices, just after ten o'clock, he was behind Bennison. He whispered: "Proper old worry-guts, Mr Kent is."

"He'll never change now," said Bennison.

He went ahead; Charley followed, three or four yards behind. Charley wore a bowler hat and a light grey suit, Bennison wore his usual lightweight grey; he got very hot in ordinary weight clothes.

Everything was normal. Market vans and lorries were moving along the narrow street; at one end big piles of wooden crates laden with fruit and vegetables were stacked up, waiting for collection. The faintly sickly smell of stale vegetables was wafted towards them on a light wind. A man pushed a barrow laden to over-flowing with bright yellow oranges marked *Outspan*. Another followed, with boxes of apples marked: *Australian Granny Smiths*. A small van had some boxes of bananas: *West Indies Produce,* ran the legend.

Bennison thought then as he so often did, of the curious kind of romance of the market, the ironical fact that the rough, tough, hoarse, coarse, powerful men who worked in it were virtually rubbing shoulders with people all over the world, dark-skinned, light-skinned, men and women, some working for a good wage, some for just enough to stay alive. Although he had a reasonable knowledge of the economics of the trade, he always marvelled that fruit could come so far and keep so well and be so cheap – although its cheapness was a thing about which Isobel disagreed.

He smiled at the thought of Isobel.

He saw the two men standing by the side of a partly loaded van – with some onions threatening to break a sack of red string, boxed cabbages, some sacks of potatoes. He did not pay any particular attention to them as he turned into the bank.

He went to his usual cashier, whom he had known for ten years – and yet did not really know.

"Good morning."

"Everything as usual, Mr Bennison?"

"No major changes."

"I won't keep you long."

He kept Bennison for seven minutes, during which time Charley lounged on one side, near the door. If there was a tense moment, it was when Bennison walked out with the five hundred pounds in the old leather bag, with the one pound notes, the ten shilling notes, the silver and the copper. The bag was quite heavy. He had it chained to his wrist – virtually, he was handcuffed to it; not that he ever admitted thinking that there might be the slightest need to take such a precaution.

He nodded to Charley.

He went outside.

He noticed that the van with the two men was still pulled into the kerb. Had they tyre trouble or engine trouble? Or were they waiting for more goods? Bennison thought of that idly, as he drew level with the van, and the first thing which scared him was a low whistle which came from one of the men.

Then, Charley shouted: *"Mr Ben—look out! Look—"*

Bennison half turned. A man, just behind him, was bringing something down – a weapon, something which in that split second looked like an iron bar. Bennison kicked out, but before he felt his foot land anywhere, a blow smashed on his head, and his skull seemed to split.

Behind him, Charley made a desperate effort to catch up, but a man closed in on him from a doorway. Charley saw the man's face, recognised it, saw a momentary spasm of alarm in the man's eyes. Then he caught a glimpse of the knife in the other's hand. Before he could cry out, he felt a strange, frightening, white-hot pain in his chest.

Chapter Two

The Second Look

The two men who had been standing by the side of the half empty van moved with calculated speed, knowing exactly what they had to do. They glanced fleetingly at their accomplice who had been standing in a doorway and was now attacking the guard. Luck was on their side, for only a few people were really close to the scene, and in that instant no one seemed to have any idea what was happening.

Win Marriott, the man wielding the iron bar, smashed it down on the head of the man with the money as matter-of-factly as he would use a hammer on a nail. He saw the terror in the man's grey eyes, saw them roll as unconsciousness came. Before the man fell, Marriott bent down and grabbed his legs. Mo Dorris caught the victim's shoulders at the same time. They had rehearsed this a dozen times, and timed it to perfection. Blood was already spattering Dorris, but it did not make him stop. They held the victim, Bennison, between them, swung him twice, and pitched him over the top of the crates of fruit and vegetables. They let him go. He crashed against the floor of the van, which had been left empty in the middle. At the same moment the engine roared, and the fourth member of the gang started to drive off. The two attackers swung on to the tail board and over. By that time a man was shouting: "Thief! Stop thief!"

A woman's screams were like a wail.

"*Pol-leeece,*" she cried. "*Pol-leeece!*"

A youth who looked as if he had been a Teddy Boy too long, with black shiny, oily hair and narrow trousers, made a flying leap for the truck, clutched the tail-board for a moment, and began to climb over.

Marriott smashed the iron bar on to his knuckles and he dropped off, gasping.

A man pushing a barrow of oranges, those which Bennison had seen, swung round, realised what was happening, saw the glitter in the eyes of the van driver – and pushed his cart, oranges and all, in its path. The driver wrenched his wheel. The offside wing caught the handle of the truck, and sent it careering to one side, boxes of oranges falling off, bursting the frail wood which held them in, the fruit rolling all over the road, some squashed by the wheels of the van and squirting rich juice. The man who had pushed the truck trod on one and skidded helplessly.

The van screamed round a corner.

Marriott and Dorris pulled up the tail-board, so that they could not be seen, and then bent over Bennison. Marriott now held a short, stubby knife. He stuck the knife into the thick leather of the wages bag, and worked with a sawing motion, quick, expert, effective. One cut made, he worked downwards.

Dorris was crouching and watching him, intently.

Bennison made a little moaning sound.

Blood was oozing from his head, and running into the sacks of cabbages on one side, another trickle was smearing some carrots.

Marriott stabbed with the knife again, making a third cut – and inside the bag the wads of money showed, all neatly parcelled.

"*How* much did you say it was?" Dorris demanded.

"Five thousand."

"That's not five thou'!"

"Bound to be," Marriott said. He snatched the money out and stuffed it into his pockets. "Where are we?"

Dorris, still crouching, stared at him for a long time. Marriott licked his lips, and asked more savagely: "*Where are we?*"

"That's not five thou'—"

"What the hell does it matter how much it is, we've got it, haven't we? *Where are we?*"

Bennison moaned again. Marriott looked down and saw his eyes flicker open, saw his right hand stretched out, as if to try to pull at his, Marriott's, ankle. Marriott picked up a box of apples, and smashed it down on Bennison's head and face. The box broke, the wood splintering, and apples began to roll about the floor, but Bennison lay still. Dorris was standing upright, now, and he glanced round.

"We're at Goswell Road."

"Tell Alec to slow down."

"But—"

"Tell him to slow down!"

Dorris turned away and banged on the back of the driver's cabin. Almost at once the van slackened speed. Marriott did not lower the tail-board again, but climbed over it. Dorris followed him, quickly. As they landed, the van stopped. Several people stared at them curiously, especially at Dorris, for there were splashes of blood on his face. The driver, a lad in his teens who looked rather like a girl, said:

"Got it?"

"Yeh—split up yet?"

"Later."

"Win—" Dorris began.

"See you," Marriott said.

He turned and hurried off towards the City. The youth who had driven them here turned in the opposite direction. Marriott dodged across the road, aware that a lot of people were staring at him. He got on to a Number 17 bus, rode on it for five minutes, then dropped off again and hailed a taxi. He sat back in the cab, quivering from reaction, and patting his pockets. He was feeling sick, because he knew that Dorris was right – they had done all this for a few hundred quid. He could not be sure of it, but in a mood of pessimism he thought that there was no more than three hundred pounds in his pocket – three hundred, for all that. Not a hundred apiece. The kid Alec would have to have fifty, the rest was to be split three ways.

He moistened his lips.

It hadn't been so clever, either. Now that it was over he could see the glaring weaknesses, and it was no help to think that he had planned all this. The actual scene of the robbery had been good, and the information had seemed reliable. It had come from a clerk who had once worked at Revels, but had left months ago. Marriott had watched the bank, learned the procedure which was followed every payday – but had not thought to question the amount.

Five thousand? Or five *hundred*?

Never mind how much; he should have had something laid on, a cab or a car or another van so that they could have changed vehicles. It had been a mistake to come here without transport laid on, and to rush off in three directions. He had seen at least two police helmets bobbing along the street.

He hadn't heard a police whistle, though; had he?

He got out of the taxi at the Bank, and mixed with the thick crowds of people in Lombard Street. The company of so many others gave him a feeling of security; he had always liked crowds. The more he thought about what had happened, the less worried he became. He would have heard a police whistle if one had been blown, he was sure of that, so probably four or five minutes had passed before anyone had discovered the man in the van.

He might not be discovered even now – might be still lying on the floor, all among the oranges and lemons. Spuds and carrots, more like!

Marriott began to smile broadly, and to perspire. He was a rather short, broad-shouldered man in the middle twenties, with a big face and a broad chin and surprisingly fine, pale blue eyes. His hair, always kept very short, was medium coloured, rather more brown than anything else, and his nose was short so that the nostrils showed rather noticeably. Now, he wore an old suit of brown tweed, and only his associates knew that the money was in one capacious inside pocket, taking up much of the skirt of the jacket. There might be five hundred, after all – better than a smack in the eye. The sooner he could count it the better.

He walked along more briskly, planting his feet down very squarely, as if he had nothing to fear and was ready to face the world. Twice he passed bank messengers with cash bags chained to their waists. Lucky devils, they were – but their turn would come one day! He glanced at the entrance of several big banks, and had the same kind of exhilarated feeling. It was not dampened when a policeman came along, walking slowly, looking at a motor-cycle parked in the street where there should be no parking. That was about all these bloody coppers were good for, these days; picking on parked cars and stalling around until the drivers came up.

Marriott reached Aldgate.

He took a bus which went along the Mile End Road, got off at a corner with a public house on one side and a cafe on the other, and sauntered towards the cafe. Sitting in the window was Mo Dorris. Good-o! Sitting next to Dorris was Alec Gool, the driver. *Good-o!* Only Stevens, the man who had been detailed to look after the escort, was missing. Marriott went in breezily, cocked a thumb at the thick-waisted young girl behind the counter, called: "Coffee and hamburger, toots," and sat down with the others at a window table.

"Where's Stevens?" he demanded in a whisper.

"He's okay—he phoned a message to the caff," Dorris said. "He's on the way."

"Any trouble?"

"It was easy, like the rest," young Alec Gool said. "Perfect. We knocked off the van, and after that it went as smooth as a tart's—"

Alec Gool broke off, as a man walked past the window: this was Stevens. He glanced in, then came in. There was a quality about Stevens which sometimes worried Marriott; he was too big for his boots. Tall, with sharp features and rather supercilious expression, he looked round as if to say that he was above this kind of cafe, with the buns and sandwiches under plastic covers, the urns bubbling, the hot dogs and the hamburgers waiting to be cooked, the cheap soft drinks, the cheap calendars and posters showing bosomy girls, the old and dirty oilcloth, the plastic covered tables which were never quite clean.

He came and sat down.

"How much?" he demanded.

"Haven't had a chance to count," said Marriott.

"Well, what's stopping you?"

"No hurry," Marriott said. He leaned back on his chair, so that it looked almost as if he would fall backwards. His eyes were narrowed, and he consciously challenged Stevens. To himself, he was saying: there's got to be a showdown sooner or later. He's got to know who's boss. He hoped that this showed in his eyes.

"About four hundred quid," Dorris said.

Stevens caught his breath. *"How* much?"

"Four hundred nicker."

"But you said—"

"So we said it would be five thou'," interrupted Marriott. He spoke very slowly and deliberately, his thoughts still running on the same lines: this man had to know who was the boss. "He didn't pick up much today. I haven't counted it yet but it might be five hundred. That's the lot."

Stevens was staring at him. Marriott suddenly licked his lips. Dorris said, *"What's up?"* and stopped. Young Alec was watching both men, eyes darting to and fro. He was thin faced, curly haired, rather aesthetic-looking, and he had long fingers with beautifully manicured nails, and a good complexion. His harsh, Cockney voice took strangers by surprise and filled some of them with disappointment.

"What are you looking at me like that for?" Marriott demanded.

"Where's the rest?"

"I've told you—"

"There were five thousand pounds in that bag."

"Not on your life," Dorris said. "I saw him cut it open. I know."

"Pack it in," said Alec Gool. "The broad's coming." He waited until the girl placed cups of coffee and hamburgers on the table, winked into her coarse, blotchy face, and waited for her to go. All this time Marriott and Stevens were staring at each other, and Marriott found his breath getting short.

"The newspapers will tell us how much it was," Alec put in. "Win wouldn't try anything. He knows he'd be found out!"

"You said five thousand," Stevens repeated.

"It—it must have been a mistake. It must have been—"

"*Mistake*," Stevens echoed in a grating whisper.

"The—the chap who told me *said* five grand. That's five thou', isn't it?"

"Let's see it," said Stevens. "Come on, let's see it."

There was a small back room, off a passage leading to the lavatories. They crowded into the room, and Marriott took out the money. The one pound notes were in packs of twenty-five pounds; so were the ten shilling notes. In all, there was four hundred and seventy-five pounds, and at the bottom of the bag was the list of instructions which Bennison had given to the cashier at the bank: a level five hundred pounds.

"So that's all," Stevens said, stonily.

"I told you it was," Marriott said. He paused, as if expecting Stevens to start talking about the misinformation, but hurried on when Stevens kept silent. "The rest was silver and copper, see. Didn't want me to bring that with me, did you?" He had the money back in his pocket. "Fifty for Alec—"

"Seventy-five," said Alec Gool, quickly. "Seventy-five for me and a hundred and thirty-three for each of you guys, and a quid for the meal. I couldn't say fairer than that, could I?"

No one argued.

Quickly, Marriott counted the money; as quickly, each man tucked it away. When they had finished the share out they went back for coffee and more food. Soon Marriott and Dorris went off together.

An hour later, Alec and Stevens left, also together, the youngest and the oldest of the foursome, a lad of seventeen or eighteen and a man in his middle forties.

"That pair won't get anywhere," Alec said, with complete assurance. "They're dead beats already. Anyone who could get five thousand and five hundred mixed up wants his head examined. But you and me, Steve—we got a future."

The older man made no comment.

They walked towards the junction of Whitechapel and Commercial Roads, where newspapermen were calling, and placards were showing up in the sunlight. By one of these, Marriott and Dorris were standing, buying a paper.

The other two walked past, but as they did so, they read:

"*Bank Raid Murder.*"

"So you killed him," Alec said. He darted a quick, almost admiring glance at Stevens.

"So you killed him," Dorris muttered to Marriott, half under his breath.

"He wasn't dead! Stevens must—" Marriott broke off, moistened his lips, and then put his hand inside his pocket, to touch his hundred and thirty-three pounds.

"Well, one of them's dead," Dorris declared, in the same half audible voice. "So it's a murder rap."

"Don't lose your nerve," Marriott said. "No one knows who it was. We've just got to keep our nerve, that's all. Nothing will go wrong, don't you worry."

"If you ask me, plenty's gone wrong," Dorris said. "We've got some thinking to do."

"While I'm around, let me do the thinking," ordered Marriott.

As he spoke, he glanced round, but Stevens and Alec were out of sight. Standing and looking at the placard was a policeman.

Chapter Three

The Third Look

Chief Superintendent Roger West, of New Scotland Yard, was having a slacker day than usual. The years had taught him the value of taking every job that came his way as calmly and unhurriedly as possible; ten minutes' thought at the beginning of an investigation could save a lot of wasted time later.

In his early forties, he was the youngest senior ranking detective in the Criminal Investigation Department of the Metropolitan Police. Years ago, when he had been the youngest inspector, some of his colleagues had resented his speedy promotion, but no one resented him now. He still had the looks which had earned him the soubriquet "Handsome" and was still known by most people at the Yard simply as "Handsome" West, but there was no longer the slightest hint of sour grapes about the use of that nickname.

He had a small office overlooking the Thames, preferring it to a larger room without a river and embankment view. His desk was in one corner. Squeezed into another, behind the door, was a much smaller desk – that of Chief Inspector Cope, Roger's chief *aide*. Cope was out, probably snatching a cup of tea or coffee in the canteen. His desk was tidy, and all his work as up to date as C.I.D. work could be. There were always cases pending.

On the mantelpiece, where in the winter a small fire always glowed despite the big radiators, were some reference books and, on one side, a large photograph – of a woman and two boys. The boys were young, in the picture, no more than eight or nine, and the woman looked very young, too; in the late twenties, perhaps. Now and again, when deeply involved in a case, Roger would glance up at this photograph of his wife and two sons, give a half smile, and get back to the job in hand.

At that moment he had never heard of the Bennisons; although his own family had a lot in common with them. It was half past eleven on the Friday morning and he was wondering whether he would be able to take the Saturday off and make it a full week-end. He had managed two already this summer. He knew that the boys had a full programme of sports – tennis and swimming mostly – and now, at the age of eighteen and seventeen, they could take care of themselves. If he could get down to the coast for a couple of days with Janet, it would set them up for weeks. Finding a hotel would be a problem, but the Brighton Police had worked miracles for him before. He liked Brighton. In some ways, it seemed to him more truly London's seaside than Southend, which was East London's resort.

The door opened, and Cope came in. Cope was a big, weighty, heavy-looking man, with a round, rather doleful face, almost bull-like in his expression. He had thinning black hair, a prominent, beaky nose, deep-set eyes which were so dark blue they were almost black.

"Heard about that Covent Garden job?"

"A bit about it," said Roger.

"They've found the van."

"Any sign of the missing man?"

"There's a sign of him all right," said Cope. He squeezed between the wall and his desk, and sat down. He was a man always likely to complain when there was nothing to complain about, and yet bore legitimate grievances – such as the size of his living space in this office – with saint-like long-suffering. "Bashed about badly. Proper mess."

Roger didn't speak.

"One dead, one on the danger list—not a bad score," Cope went on. He brought a sheet of paper to Roger's desk. "Meant to give this to you," he said with annoyance. "Shall I read it out?"

Roger stood up. News of murder, news of men being beaten to the point of death, always created restlessness and the beginning of anger in him, and he was glad to go to the window, then come back to pick up the sheet of paper. It was a teleprint message, put out by the Information Room, and for the first time he saw the name Bennison.

"Second victim of Covent Garden bank robbery found in a van stolen from Medley Brothers there, early this morning. The van was on loan to Medley Brothers. Victim's name: Paul Bennison, of 35, Acacia Avenue, Wimbledon. Aged 39. Married, wife named Isobel, aged 38. Three children, one girl 17. Bennison taken to Charing Cross Hospital to undergo emergency operation for head and face injuries. No report of his condition yet available."

Roger, standing in front of Cope's desk, read this very slowly. Cope was breathing heavily; he suffered a little from sinus.

"Nasty," he said.

Roger found himself thinking: *Wife, three children.*

"What about the messenger, the man named Charley Blake?"

"Widower," Cope replied. "One married daughter, who lives in Canada. He lived at a working men's hostel, and spent most of his spare time watching television or football matches."

In a queer way, Roger was relieved; at least the death of the man who had escorted Bennison to and from the bank was likely to cause no deep immediate grief, no one would really suffer. Bennison was different.

"Who's going to handle this job?" asked Cope.

"I don't know," said Roger.

"That flicking conference," Cope remarked, and pulled some papers towards him.

There was a conference of Assistant Commissioners and Commanders that morning, and decisions were apt to be made slowly. The Division was covering the initial investigations into the crimes, of course, and was not likely to miss much, but this would undoubtedly be a job for one of the Yard's senior men, and Roger knew that he was the most likely. So he spent fifteen minutes reading through the early reports.

Among them was an eye-witness account of the attack on the guard, Blake. The eye-witness was a middle-aged porter, who had been carrying a pile of baskets on his head. He had been on the other side of the road.

"This chap come straight out of the doorway and I see him take the knife out of his belt. He didn't mean to miss. He stabbed upwards, clean through the ribs. I knew the poor devil was done for before he hit the ground. All over in a flash, it was."

Roger let this sink into the back of his mind while he considered the other statements. One thing was constant: the speed with which the attack had been carried out. A woman who had chanced to be looking out of an office window on the first floor of the building next to the bank, said:

"I could hardly believe my eyes. I saw one man, rather short and thickset I thought, strike his victim on the head with a bar of something—I think it was angle iron, my husband uses angle iron sometimes when building garages, and I know what it looks like. Then he seemed to pull his victim backwards while the other man snatched at his legs. There was hardly a pause before they swung him into the van, as if he were a sack of potatoes. I can still hear the thud as he hit the floor. The van began to move almost at once, and the two assailants jumped into the back. Then the van knocked over a truck of oranges, and disappeared round the corner."

The porter who had been pushing away a truckload of oranges, on his way to supply some barrow boys, said simply:

"I didn't see the attack but I heard shouting and saw the getaway lorry. I pushed my truck at the driver, but he swerved and only caught it by the handle. Lost me ten quids' worth of oranges but I'd do it again if I had to."

There were other witnesses, including a youth who said he "saw something was up" and jumped on to the back of the lorry, "but someone smacked a bloody great bar of iron on my hand".

There were less positive reports about the guard's murderer, the man with a knife. The first man and the woman from the window had seen most – and were the two most likely to have seen the faces of the three men involved. No one appeared to have noticed the driver of the lorry.

There was a note about that.

"The lorry belonged to Medley Brothers of West Ham. It was on loan to Medleys of Covent Garden, and had not been used that morning. It would have been driven back to West Ham later. The driver was having his lunch at the time of the theft."

"We could do with a word with that driver, too," Roger said *sotto voce.*

"Wassat?" asked Cope.

"Forget it."

"Talking to yourself, first sign that is," said Cope, bode-fully. He looked up and grinned. "Want to handle this job, don't you?"

"I do and I don't," replied Roger, quite truthfully.

As he finished, one of the two telephones on his desk rang and he picked it up with the swift movement which came of long practice.

"West."

"Oh, Handsome." This was Campbell, the newly promoted Deputy Commander of the Criminal Investigation Department. The Commander was on holiday and the Assistant Commissioner had been called to Paris on an *Interpol* job, so Campbell was in charge. "You haven't got any big job on, have you?"

"Not yet," Roger said.

Campbell laughed.

"You're right – I'm going to put a stop to that. The Covent Garden job. Will you have a quick look at it and let me know what you make of it by this afternoon? The Old Man is a bit worried." The "Old

Man" was the Commissioner, the head of the Metropolitan Police, and if he took a personal interest in any investigation, it meant that everyone had to be high on their toes. "There have been so many of these wage snatch jobs."

"I'll have a go at it," Roger said.

"Give it priority, won't you?"

Roger winked across at Cope.

"I'll see the three eye-witnesses whose statements seem as if they might be some good before the morning's out—they're all over at West Central., I'll check with the firm who employed Bennison—Revel & Son. I can't quite understand why the attacker hiding in a doorway used a knife on the escort named Blake. I should have thought that a clout over the head would have been enough – and then it wouldn't have been a murder rap. As it is, we'll be able to hang the man who used the knife, and I for one—"

"*Kamerad,*" Campbell said, laughing.

He rang off.

"So you've got it," Cope said gloomily. "That means I won't be able to leave the office. Chained to a desk, that's me. Worse than clink. Who'd be a copper?"

"Find out where Bennison lives, will you?" Roger said. "I mean, the kind of district. Get in touch with the Division, get all details you can about his family, age of the children and that kind of thing. I want a complete dossier on the dead man, too. And if you're looking for a job after that—"

"Put a sock in it," growled Cope. He picked up a telephone and said into it: "Mr West's on his way. Send his car and a driver round to the front, will you?"

Roger nodded thanks as he picked up his murder bag, a square box-like case, which was always kept ready. As the door swung to behind him and he walked along the bleak, bare passages towards the lift, he thought half-amusedly, half-sombrely of his own and Campbell's reactions; of Cope's, too. Here was tragedy, swift and vicious. Men struck down in the course of doing their job, cold-blooded and ruthless killers at work. Here was a woman and her family suddenly plunged into anxiety and fear, and perhaps soon to lose the man about whom their world was built-and the Yard joked. The Yard had to joke. To show one's feelings, even to *feel* deeply, would only get in the way of their job.

Nothing must get in the way of it; he wanted that killer; he wanted all four of the men concerned.

Chapter Four

Disquiet

The body had been taken away from the scene of the murder, but the police had cordoned off part of the pavement and of the roadway. Only one-way traffic was possible, much to the disgust of the drivers of fruit and vegetable lorries and small vans, even to the disgust of the porters wheeling trucks. To make it worse, a hundred or more people were on the other side of the road, gawping. Three youngish girls had climbed up on top of a big trailer which was loaded with produce, and were standing up, pointing, gesticulating, taking photographs. Uniformed police were moving the crowd along as best they could. Two or three plainclothes men from the Division were mixing with the crowd, and a tall, thin, raffish-looking individual named Simpson was bending over the chalk lines which indicated the spot where the body had been found. More chalk lines showed the position of the stolen lorry and approximately where the two men had stood when they had attacked Bennison.

Simpson was a sniffer.

"They told me you'd be along, Handsome," he said. "Can't say I'm sorry to see you. Quicker we can let traffic move along here the better. They'll start pelting us with bad oranges soon."

"All the photographing done?" asked Roger.

"Yes."

"Swept the pavement and the road?"

"I can lay it on whenever you like," said Simpson.

"Thanks." Roger went down on one knee, and studied the smaller chalk marks. Simpson, recently promoted Chief Inspector, was as good as anyone at the Divisions and better than most. He had marked wherever there were spots of blood, footprints, heel prints, anything at all the slightest degree unusual. There was a fresh scar on the pavement, for instance, obviously made by something hard. It was marked: *"Weapon used in attack may have struck here—it fell from the assailant's hand."* There were a dozen other little notes, all made on slips of paper and sealed in plastic containers which were stuck to the ground.

As he went on with the check, Roger asked questions, and the answers were all as he expected. The Divisional Police Surgeon had been and pronounced Blake dead … some prints of photographs should be along within the hour … the three witnesses whose statements he had picked out were all available. Simpson had not kept them away from their work but arranged that they could be available for questioning the moment they were wanted. Three other eye-witnesses had now come forward but none of them appeared to have seen as much as the three already known.

"But I'd have a word with them, Handsome."

"Yes," Roger said. He straightened up. "I think we can take the barricade away now—you obviously haven't missed anything."

"I'll get the place swept up and vacuumed," Simpson said. "You going to see those eye-witnesses?"

"I'll see the bank people first, and then the office staff at Bennison's place," Roger said. He wondered how Bennison was. The hospital was only a few minutes away from here, and it might be a good idea to go in and see him. "Anyone at Bennison's side?"

"What do *you* think?"

Roger smiled.

"But he won't be able to talk for a couple of days at least," Simpson gloomed.

The bank officials were troubled, but could not help very much. It was true that Mr Bennison collected five hundred pounds or so every week, but he had never been careless. It was a comparatively small sum for four men to aim at. Any one of the bank staff knew how regularly the money was collected, of course, and presumably a lot of other people could have known. This particular morning one of the two escorts had not turned up – the bank officials did not know why.

"It's a small sum all right," Roger said. "Do you have any large regular payments which go out on a Friday?"

The Bank Manager, middle-aged, a little slow speaking, perhaps because he was so worried, admitted that there were.

"We have four wages accounts of over two thousand pounds which are drawn every Friday," he said. "Most of them are drawn on Thursdays these days, but …"

"Will you let me have the details of the accounts?" Roger interrupted.

"I'll have a list and all additional information typed out for you."

"Thanks," said Roger.

He walked along towards Revel & Son's premises. Two vacuum cleaners were buzzing, each of them running off a battery in a car, and two plainclothes men were sweeping the pavement and the kerb, and putting the dust, straw, pieces of paper, straws from horse droppings, tobacco shreds, bus tickets, orange peel, matches, everything they could find, into large plastic bags. Someone on the other side of the road was using a cine camera – it was a B.B.C. Television Unit. A man called out: "Mr West—can you spare a moment?"

Roger, knowing he was being photographed, put on a tight-lipped smile and waited. A man with a microphone came up.

"Are you in charge of the investigation into this shocking crime, Mr West?"

"I'm working with the West Central Division—and with Chief Inspector Simpson," Roger said. Simpson was keeping out of range; Roger beckoned him, and he gave a harsh sniff and came near quickly enough. The camera was busy all the time, and amateur photographers were clicking away.

"Have you any clues yet, Mr West?"

"We've got very good descriptions of at least three of the men involved."

"Was any one of them known to the Yard?"

"If they're known to *Records,* we'll soon have them."

"Is it true that the amount stolen was five hundred pounds?"

"About that amount, yes."

"Is it true that the lorry used had been stolen?"

"As far as I know, yes."

"Have you had any further news of the second victim—Mr Paul Bennison?"

"I hope to have, soon," Roger said. "And yes—I do hope for quick results! That's provided I can get on to the job quickly." He grinned, the man with the microphone smiled, Roger said in an aside to Simpson: "Give 'em details of what you've done so far." He walked on, leaving a highly gratified Simpson. Roger found two uniformed policemen near the open doorway of Revel & Son, and was taken up the narrow, wooden staircase. There was no lift and the landings were dark and gloomy. At last he reached the top floor, where walls had been knocked down, years ago, to make one large office. The manager, named Kent, was suffering severely from shock. He had some difficulty in keeping his lips steady, and there was a tremor in his hands. He obviously felt responsible because he had not made sure that a third man had gone with Bennison and the escort.

"I've always been s-s-s-so careful, never b-b-b-b-believed in taking chances—"

Roger treated him as gently as he could.

A middle-aged woman with straight hair and a fringe gave him all the information he asked for about the dead man – and about the other escort, a messenger who had been taken ill, according to his wife.

Roger made a note of his name: Harry Myers, with an address in Kensal Green.

Next, Roger started trying to find out who knew about the regular visit to the bank, and learned what he had feared – everyone knew. Thirty-one members of the weekly wage staff, eleven of the office, salaried staff – and probably a lot of temporary workers, messengers who came in and out with orders or to collect goods. At least seventy-five people knew, and the difficulty of finding out which one, if any, had given the information to the criminals was almost insuperable.

Most inquiries looked like this in the beginning, but the blank wall had seldom seemed as high and unclimbable as this time. Roger reminded himself that he had three eye-witnesses and three descriptions of men who were wanted; he was being pessimistic for the sake of it.

Something about this case filled him with disquiet.

He tried to analyse his reasons as he kept asking questions, but didn't get very far. When he had finished with Kent and the office staff, and was about to leave the premises, a very old man with snowy white hair and a cherry pink skin appeared. He was leaning on a stick and looked as fragile as old china.

"This is Mr Revel, sir," the secretary said, in a subdued voice.

"You're West, aren't you?" The old man's voice was not as frail as his body.

"Yes, Mr Revel."

"I want you to know that I will leave nothing undone, nothing at all, to find this murderer. I am prepared to offer a reward of five thousand pounds ..."

"I wouldn't just yet," Roger said, when Revel had finished. "We may get results quickly without that. If we do—" he checked himself from saying that the five thousand pounds might be much more useful for the Bennisons. The man and the policeman too often overlapped. "We shan't waste any time, I assure you."

"I should hope not," said Revel. His eyes looked tired, and watered a little; there was a speck of white "sleep" in the corners. He leaned heavily on his stick as if afraid of falling, without it. "I ask you to think of the side effects of this—this wicked crime. Bennison's family, for instance. My manager, Mr Kent, he—he has had a terrible shock. I've never seen such a change in a man. You are looking for very wicked men, Superintendent."

"Yes," said Roger. "I know."

Wicked men –

Issues were simple for some of the old people, for the Revels of this world. When had the word "wicked" gone out of date?

Roger went out. The sweeping up had finished and traffic was flowing in both directions now. The TV unit had gone, and so had most of the crowd on the other side of the road. It was getting very warm, the sun was high and the mist all gone.

Simpson was coming out of the bank, carrying an envelope.

"The bank manager's list," he said.

"Thanks," Roger took it. "We'll need to keep all of these firms in mind, the attack might have been intended for one of their cashiers, not Revel's." He slid into the car which was parked nearby, and the driver came hurrying from a corner. "I'm not going anywhere yet," Roger said, and flicked on the two-way radio. "Superintendent West calling … Give me my office, please."

Cope's voice soon sounded, very distorted.

"Get in touch with Kensal Green, have a man go to see a Harry Myers, at …" Roger gave the address. "Myers was the messenger escort who didn't turn up. Check if he's really ill, or whether that could have been faked."

"Right," said Cope.

"I'm sending round a list of other firms who draw their wages money from the same bank," Roger said. "Telephone all of them, and ask if there's the slightest reason for any of them to think that their messengers might have been the target this morning. Just get them started – I'll go and see them as soon as I can. I'd like to have the fullest story possible when I get there."

"Right," said Cope.

"Anything more in?" asked Roger.

"Nope."

"Bennison?"

"His wife's at the hospital. He's still on the operating table."

"I see," said Roger.

He rang off, got out, and told Simpson what little there was to report. It was wise to work closely with a Divisional man, as well as with the Press and the TV authorities. He was wondering what he had left undone, and then realised that he had not yet seen any of the eye-witnesses.

First he saw the porter whose truck of oranges had suffered. He was a short, sturdy, elderly man with close-clipped iron-grey hair, and the look of the old soldier about him; he made his statement as if he were before the Commanding Officer. There was nothing to add.

"Sorry about your oranges," Roger said.

"No need to worry about that any more, sir. Mr Revel made it up to me."

"Oh," said Roger. "That's good." After a pause he added: "Do you know Mr Revel?"

"Everyone in the market knows him," declared the porter. "Been around here a lot longer than most of us."

"Yes, of course," said Roger.

Mrs Gossard, the woman clerk who had seen the attack, was inclined to be over talkative, but very positive, and her descriptions of the two men who had attacked Bennison and flung him into the lorry were very precise. In a curious way, her prolixity combined with matter-of-factness gave the incident an additional touch of horror, particularly as she said: "I do assure you, Superintendent, I have never in all my life heard a sound like the sound of that poor man when he hit the floor of that lorry. It was enough to break every bone in his body. I hope I never hear anything like it again."

"I certainly hope not, too," Roger said.

The porter whose eye-witness account he had read first, was ready to go home, and waiting about at one of the fruit wholesalers' in the market. He was a casual worker, a big, husky, black-haired man who badly needed a shave. A tooth was missing on the right hand side of his mouth, and his other teeth were uneven, although very white. In spite of the heat, he wore a choker, tightly-knotted, a reefer jacket and a pair of blue serge trousers. There was something of the manner of a sailor about him – almost a piratical air. He was sitting on a pile of boxes and the roller shutters of the shop were almost on a level with his head. The shop, *Green & Co.*, specialised in produce from South Africa.

The porter's name was Calwin.

He repeated his story with gusto, but without standing up – his manner seemed to say that he wasn't going to stand up for any policeman; it was a kind of controlled truculence.

"Thanks," said Roger, briskly. "Now, let's see what you missed, as well as what you saw. Did you—?"

"I didn't miss anything!"

"You didn't?"

"No, I never. I've told you more'n one of your flat foots would, in the circs." The man stayed seated, now downright truculent and almost aggressive.

"Not on your life," Roger said. "Our chaps are trained to observe. What—?"

"Are you telling me I didn't keep my eyes open?" Calwin rose slowly to his feet. Roger noticed that he had very big but well-kept hands. "Listen, copper—"

"Did you see the knife?"

"You calling me a liar?"

"Did you get a good view of it?"

"I've *told* you I did."

"What hand was it in?"

"Eh?"

"What hand was it in—his right or his left?"

"His—his *right*, of course."

"Sure?"

"What?"

"Are you *sure?*"

The porter, half a head taller than Roger, who was six feet plus, looked down, frowning. He had small, clear brown eyes, and a very hardy weathered complexion. He wrinkled his nose, then put his finger to a nostril, and scratched. There was a silence which seemed to last for a long time, before he answered: "Yep. Right hand."

"Thanks. What pocket did he take it out of?"

"He took it out of his *belt*—and don't ask me whether I'm sure or not. I *am* sure."

"Good. How long was the blade?"

"Eh?"

"How long was the blade?"

The porter said thoughtfully: "Proper artful, aincha? I'd say six inches, but it's only a guess. I only got a glimpse of it. Don't expect me to have photographic eyes, do you?"

"Yours aren't too bad," Roger conceded, and grinned. "Let's see if I've got it right. The knife was in the killer's belt. He used his right hand. He waited for the messenger to draw level, then jumped him, drawing the knife out, and stabbing him so quickly that you didn't have a chance to see the knife very clearly. You only caught a glimpse of the blade."

"That's right." Calwin looked wary, as if not sure exactly what this was leading up to. "Just a silver flash, that was all. I saw it go in." He was not quite so matter of fact as he tried to make out.

Roger glanced round, espied a sliver of wood about the size of a carving knife, leaned across and held it out to the man.

"Show me, will you?"

"Listen, what's so important?"

"Just show me, and I'll tell you."

The big man scowled, and was obviously puzzled and wary. A small man in a light grey overcheck suit and a bowler hat watched intently from the back of the shop. Calwin moved a little sheepishly to one side, between two piles of crates.

"He was in the shop doorway, like this, see—you going to be the victim?"

Roger moved. "Yes."

"Go over there a bit—that's right." Calwin waved. "Now take three steps forward, see? ... As you're stepping out, you bellow something, what was it? ... Look out, that's it, look out. You're staring at Bennison, see, and the cove who's attacking him. *Look out!* you bellow, to warn Bennison. Then this cove took out 'is knife—"

Calwin jumped out, snatching the stick of wood from under his coat and stabbing in one swift, sweeping movement. The point of the sliver actually pressed into Roger's ribs, and he felt a scratch of pain. Calwin drew his hand back quickly, and drew away.

"You're no actor," he jeered. "You ought to have collapsed by now. That's exactly—"

He broke off.

Roger saw Simpson standing just in front of the shop, the top of his head hidden by the shutters. With him was a woman, half a head shorter, fair-haired, attractive in a wholesome way, but with no colour in her cheeks and a curious brightness in her eyes. Her hands were clenched by her sides. He realised, even before Simpson told him, that this was Mrs Bennison.

Chapter Five

The Wife

As he moved towards them, ducking under the half-closed shutters, Roger thought: Bennison's dead. The woman looked up into his face without speaking, and he had a strange feeling – that she was looking for something which she did not expect to find. Simpson coughed, and said: "Mrs Bennison came along to see Mr Kent. She would like a word with you, Superintendent."

"*Her*," breathed Calwin.

Roger held out his hand. "I can't tell you how sorry I am." As he spoke, he wondered almost desperately if he were right, if he had to condole. Until he was told what had happened, he could say nothing about it. "I intended to see you later in the day."

She took his hand; hers was cold, and her grip like a spasm.

"After I'd been to see your husband," Roger went on.

She didn't answer. Simpson seemed struck dumb, the fool. *Had* Bennison died? Had his death brought her here? Had it put the glitter in this woman's eyes and robbed her cheeks of colour?

The little man in the shop called: "Would you like to use my office?"

Mrs Bennison let her hand stay icy in Roger's for what seemed a long time, until he was almost embarrassed. Then she snatched it away.

"If you would like to sit down—"

"I must go home, before my children get back from school," she said. "I wanted to say—"

Roger had to interrupt: "How is Mr Bennison?" He glanced at Simpson, looking for a hint as to whether this was the wrong thing to say, but Simpson gave him no clue.

"The doctors say they won't know until this time tomorrow whether he will live," Mrs Bennison answered. Her voice was low-pitched, still controlled. "Why did you let it happen?"

"*Let* it," Calwin echoed, in a loud whisper.

"I don't quite understand you," Roger said, but he was afraid that he did.

"I should have thought it was quite simple," said Mrs Bennison. "This kind of vicious attack is a commonplace today. It happens two, three, four, sometimes as many as a dozen times a week. Why don't the police stop it?" When Roger made no attempt to give an immediate answer, she went on in a higher-pitched voice: "Why do you allow it to go on and on? Don't you realise what happens when a crime like this is committed? Don't you realise that even if my husband does recover, he may be—crippled." She choked. "He may be blinded. He may never be the same man again. Can you imagine what the effect of that would be on my children? Or on me?"

Her voice was beginning to quiver, as her self-restraint began to fail.

The easy, the obvious thing would be a platitude, rather like a gentle pat on the shoulder, or a momentary clasp of her hand or her arm. She was looking at him fixedly, it seemed as if only the two of them were here, although traffic passed and people walked by; and a policeman hovered.

"This isn't a game," Mrs Bennison said hoarsely. "It isn't play acting."

She had seen what Roger and Calwin had been attempting to reconstruct, of course, and that had helped to create this attitude, had helped to stiffen her resolve; but now her voice was quivering much more.

"A long time ago, Mrs Bennison, when I was much younger," Roger said at last, "I was investigating a case against a particularly dangerous criminal, a man who really stopped at nothing to get what he wanted, and to escape from the police. Among the things he did was to take away one of my sons—then a lad of about your younger son's age." He paused, before adding very gently: "I spent three days, going over the actual circumstances of the kidnapping—trying to reconstruct it time and time again, because I believed that it was the only way to help to find my son, and also to find the criminal. It did."

Before he had finished, tears were spilling down Isobel Bennison's cheeks.

"Will you take Mrs Bennison to my car?" Roger asked Simpson. "I'll drive her home. I won't be long."

Her home was very much as he had expected, and like his own in Bell Street, Chelsea. There was a garage, on the left, with crazy-paving wheel paths leading to it from the double gates. A diagonal path led to the front door. The house was about the same period as his – the middle-twenties- but this was built of yellow brick, whereas his was of weathered red. The roof was of red tiles, like his. The lawn was beautifully kept, and the flower beds showed the work of a gardening enthusiast. He could almost hear himself saying to Janet, his wife, that he would cut the back lawn tonight.

It was half past two.

He did not know whether to believe her, but Mrs Bennison had said that she had had some sandwiches and coffee at the hospital. Roger had let her talk on the way here, driving himself and sending his man back to the Yard. All the shock, all the horror, all the buried fears of the last ten years had come to the surface. Time and time again she had said:

"… I was always afraid of something like this, but Paul laughed at me, and I tried not to talk about it too often. I hated Friday. Every time I saw a story about a wages snatch or a bank robbery, I felt as if he was the victim. I wondered what I would feel if I were the victim's wife, what it would be like if my children were orphaned."

She was steadier, now. As she opened the front door two women came hurrying in from across the road. A small crowd of people were gathered near, and an elegant young man with a camera appeared from the back garden.

"Isobel, my dear—"

"How *is* Paul?"

"Just one *moment*, please."

"How anyone can be so *heartless?*"

Soon, they were inside, the two women following Roger and Mrs Bennison. The crowd was being kept back by a policeman, and Roger thought fleetingly that the man would soon need reinforcements. Mrs Bennison introduced her neighbours: a Mrs Beaumant and a Mrs Abbott. There were eager offers to look after the children, to take them into their homes; Isobel wasn't to worry. How *was* Paul?

"They say there is a good chance," Mrs Bennison announced, her voice quivering again. "Mr West—"

"I'll go straight to the Yard and find out, and I will tell you exactly how your husband is," Roger promised. "If I can do anything at all to help, just let me know." He didn't shake hands, but went out, glad that the neighbours were so quick off the ball and so good; he shouldn't be surprised, most neighbours were.

The elegant young man had his camera poised.

"Just one moment, please."

One day, some hysterical woman or some crazed man would smash that camera, now thrust forward with such insistence.

Roger had a word with the two policemen now on duty, hearing two lads say excitedly: "That's Handsome *West.*" He went back to his car and drove off slowly.

Once on his own, he could think, but the thinking was mostly a kind of brooding, of letting thoughts run through his mind. When Mrs Bennison had said: "Why did you let it happen?" in that bitter way, she had stabbed a metaphorical knife into his mind. The accusation was wickedly unfair of course – here he was, thinking "wicked" again – yet so understandable. None of the general public could understand the odds the police were up against. Even today, since the pay increase had brought the establishment nearer to normal, it was like trying to tell in advance which one of a handful of tossed pebbles would hit a certain spot.

He had once calculated that there were thirty thousand firms in the Metropolitan Police area, all drawing wages on Thursday or Friday. The number which paid by cheques was still negligible; both firms and workers seemed to have some prejudice against it. Thirty thousand wages bags – and possibly, *possibly*, ten snatches in a week. There simply wasn't any way of making sure that some did not succeed. There was no way of watching every one all the time. There was little anyone could do, except the big companies with their armoured vans and security men, beyond taking normal precautions. Revel & Son had taken as many as most.

There simply wasn't a way, not one yet discovered anyhow, of making sure that such crimes were not committed. The one thing the police could do was to find the criminals quickly. He had to. From the beginning, there had been something special about this case, and he believed he knew what it was: the amount of money stolen had been so small, comparatively – it had shown how vulnerable every single wage collector was. Now he had to show the criminals how vulnerable they were. He felt a sense of dedication.

His mind was buzzing with the things he had to do. He pulled off the main road, switched on a small tape recorder which ran off a battery, and dictated notes swiftly: Check Harry Myers – the absent guard.

Check other firms who draw their wages from the same bank every Friday.

Get descriptions of the three men out to the Divisions and Home Counties today.

Have a try to reconstruct the faces.

Check the West Ham company whose van was stolen.

Check contents of the plastic bags – the sweepings from the scene of the crime.

He wanted to press on urgently with each of these at once, but first had to make sure that he forgot nothing. He finished the notes, and drove to the Yard. He had a clear run, for the rush hour was still a little way off. He hurried up to his office to find Cope putting down the telephone.

"Well, that's one definite thing," he reflected. "Harry Myers is in bed with 'flu all right—I've just talked to his doctor. No fake there." As Roger crossed to his own desk, Cope went on: "And we've checked the West Ham firm over the stolen lorry. No doubt it was stolen—it was reported to the Divisional chaps half an hour before the job was done in Covent Garden, but as it was on loan, and didn't have Medley's name on, it was difficult to trace. The driver was having lunch."

"That early?"

"A market man often has lunch at our breakfast time. We just want those four, Handsome. No doubt about that."

"We'll get 'em," Roger said. The remark was almost mechanical, and the kind of banal comment which he often criticised in others. Cope didn't seem to notice it. "Anything in from the hospital?"

"No. But Simister says will you call him."

Simister was a fairly new Home Office pathologist with a growing reputation, that curious mixture of doctor, surgeon, research worker and detective which makes the great pathologists. Roger did not know him well as an individual, but respected what he knew of his work. He hesitated between calling the hospital or Simister, and plumped for the medical man, who was up in the laboratory.

"Oh, yes, West." In manner, Simister was always a little aloof, as if not quite sure of himself – unless it was a kind of snobbery. If it was, that would soon be rubbed off by contact with Yard men. "I have the report on the man Blake—the Covent Garden murder. There are one or two points which I think we should talk about."

"Whenever you like," Roger said.

"Will you come up to me?"

"I'll be up in ten minutes," promised Roger. He put down the receiver, and lifted it again almost at once, calling Campbell, whose secretary answered.

"Mr Campbell is with the Commissioner, Mr West."

"Tell him I called, will you?"

"Yes, Mr West. I wonder if—" The secretary, a woman in her early fifties, did not ring off at once. "You won't think me an old busybody if I tell you that the Commissioner seems very worried indeed about this wages snatch, will you? Apparently he spent some time with the Home Secretary this morning, and there are some repercussions in Parliament. The thing is—I'm *not* talking out of turn, am I?"

"Right in turn, and I can't tell you how much I appreciate it."

"I hoped that was how you would feel. The situation, as I understand it, is that there is a strong feeling among members of Parliament that now the police are practically at full strength there shouldn't be so much of this kind of crime. Some kind of protection should be organised. It's bad luck that the trouble's blown up over this case."

"Yes, very," said Roger. "Keep in touch with any more ominous signs, won't you?"

"Of course."

"I really appreciate it," Roger said, and hung up.

"If you ask me," said Cope, rubbing the bridge of his nose, "they're making the fuss because this was a little job with a lot of repercussions. If that chap Blake hadn't been bumped off—"

"You're half right," Roger interrupted.

"What you mean is, you half agree with me," retorted Cope. But he grinned good-naturedly. "Simpson rang up from West Central and said you went home to see Mrs Bennison right. How's she taking it?"

"Better than most," Roger replied. "I'm going upstairs to the laboratory."

Simister was rather tall, lean, a little aloof in manner, and big horn-rimmed glasses added to that suggestion of aloofness. He had small, regular features and a controlled Cambridge voice, speaking most of the time without moving his lips very much. His hair was thick, black, wavy – really quite beautiful – and he had a good if rather sallow complexion. He was wearing a long white smock, the breast pocket packed with pens and pencils. When Roger stepped into his office, a small one off the main laboratory, Simister stood up.

"Thank you for coming so quickly," he said. "Would you care to see these?"

He handed over the autopsy report on Blake.

It was very straightforward, and the single knife thrust had gone straight to the heart. The actual wording of the report had a preciseness and lucidity which made it vivid. Roger read it twice, before handing it back.

"What do you make of it?" he inquired.

"It was a remarkably accurate thrust," observed Simister. "No fumbled first blow, and clean between the ribs. The victim was wearing only a thin shirt and no vest, so there was nothing to impede the blow—no buttons, no pockets containing oddments. Death was undoubtedly instantaneous. The victim was in very good condition for a man in his early sixties, very healthy indeed."

"The kind of wound we've seen before in certain particular circumstances," Roger remarked.

"I thought you would see that. The wound is typical of those caused by in-fighting between experts. I would say that you are looking for a man with a great deal of experience in using a knife at close quarters, a man who wanted to make sure that the job was finished quickly. In other words—a trained soldier, a commando, a marine—almost certainly someone with a lot of specialist training in the armed forces."

"Thanks," Roger said. "That could be very useful."

"I hope it is," said Simister. He moved to a window which overlooked the courtyard and the tops of the buildings in Whitehall; they could just make out the tanks and pipes on top of the Charing Cross Hospital building. "Do you know Semple-Smith?"

"The surgeon?"

"Yes."

"I've met him, on a case. That was some years ago."

"He said he remembered you," said Simister. "He has been operating on the other victim, Bennison."

Roger felt his body go tense.

"What does he say?"

"He thinks that Bennison will live, but is doubtful whether he will ever be wholly fit again. The head fractures are very complicated, and there is a possibility of them causing some deterioration in Bennison's mental faculties. In addition—"

"Do you mean he might go *mad?*"

"I didn't say that," said Simister, rebukingly. "Nor did Semple-Smith. But he is a surgeon of great experience, and feels that there might be this deterioration. The degree of it varies. Sometimes there is little more than inability to concentrate, sometimes the patient finds it hard to work for long stretches. There's no certainty about the outcome, but I thought you should know."

After a pause, Roger said: "Yes. Thanks. What else were you going to say?" The face of Isobel Bennison seemed to hover in front of his eyes.

"I was about to add – in addition there are other multiple fractures – particularly in the left leg and thigh, and the left arm and shoulder. As far as it is possible to judge, Bennison landed with great force on the corners of some wooden boxes. There is at least a possibility that the left leg will have to be amputated. Semple-Smith isn't doing that part of the job – Henderson is. Whatever way you look at it, Bennison is in a very bad way."

Isobel Bennison's voice seemed to ring in Roger's ears: "*Why did you let it happen?*"

"One of the problems is what to tell the wife," went on Simister, very formally. He took off his glasses, and revealed eyes which looked pale and weak. "It isn't wise or possible for Semple-Smith or Henderson to be too reassuring. On the other hand, it would be wrong to tell Bennison's wife too much—the situation may not prove to be as bad, in the long run, as looks likely now. Are you going to see Mrs Bennison?"

Roger answered slowly, painfully: "Probably."

"Then Semple-Smith and I would appreciate knowing what you think of her, as a person. How much she can take, in other words."

"I've seen her already," Roger told him. He was keenly aware of the other's intent gaze, and the weak eyes seemed to grow stronger. "She won't be satisfied with smooth reassurances. I think—" He hesitated, telling himself that this was no part of his duty, that it would be a mistake to assume any responsibility; but that woman's face still hovered. "I think I would tell her that for a week or more it's likely to be fifty-fifty whether he lives or dies. It will be better for her that way. She'll know the risk and face it. The other—"

What Simister and Semple-Smith meant, of course, was that they feared that Bennison might become an idiot. Roger felt tensed up, and icy cold.

"That's very useful," Simister said. "Semple-Smith and I are old friends. We trained together. He is to see Mrs Bennison this evening. He'll be glad of this advice."

Roger didn't speak.

After a long pause, Simister asked: "Have you any idea who did this, yet? They were a vicious gang—very vicious indeed."

"I know."

"I wouldn't like to think they were going to give a repeat performance," Simister went on.

"What makes you say that?" Roger asked sharply.

"Isn't it obvious? They got five hundred pounds, to share among four of them. Hardly a fortune, is it? I imagine that they are very disappointed, perhaps bitter and resentful about it. If they are, they may strike again very soon." When Roger didn't respond, Simister gave a little tittering laugh. "I'm afraid I'm going outside my province. But the simple psychology of men like these—"

He broke off.

"I wish we could be sure that it was so simple," Roger said, and repeated formally: "We'll soon get them."

From the way he looked, Simister was disappointed with the banality of the remark. For in truth it was a kind of *cri de coeur*. "We'll get them," meant "I've got to get them."

Chapter Six

Try Again?

"What I say," said Marriott, "is that we've got to do another job, quick. We didn't get enough from this one to lie low for a bit. How long will a hundred quid last us? Couple of weeks, if we take it easy—that's the lot."

"Might stretch it to three," said Mo Dorris.

He was the last man in London to have such a feminine name, for he was ugly, and any redeeming feature had been battered out of recognition during his early days in the ring. No one should have allowed him to become a boxer, even a chopping block, but his youthful ambitions and his vanity had persuaded him that, given the right manager, he would become a world champion. His cauliflower right ear, his broken nose, his missing teeth, and the shiny swelling over his right eye, with the scar marks of a dozen stitches, were permanent proof of the inadequacy of his managers and the incompetence of his trainers. It was some time since he had boxed, and the only legacy he had from the boxing days – apart from his appearance – was physical fitness. Even in the ring, he had been able to take it, and since then he had kept himself fit. It was almost impossible to make him cry quits.

"You agree we ought to have another go?" asked Marriott.

"I can't wait," Dorris agreed.

They were sitting in a different cafe, near the docks, late that evening. The cafe was nearly full. Blue-grey tobacco smoke was thick and stinking, teenagers chattered over coffee and eggs and chips, hamburgers and hot dogs. A juke box kept playing, on and off; now it was droning *Mac the Knife*. Three very short girls with exaggeratedly pointed breasts were at the bar, serving as waitresses, each wearing a ludicrously short skirt, well above the knee, each given the job and doing the job because she would attract the "men". Outside, the street lamps of London's dockland were just lighting up, it was half past nine.

Marriott and Dorris were in a corner, speaking in low pitched, conspiratorial voices.

"What do you think Steve will think?" asked Marriott.

"Who cares?" demanded Dorris.

"I care."

"You're the boss," said Dorris. "If you want to worry about a long streak like that, you can worry. I'm not worrying. If he hadn't used that knife—"

"He had to stop the guard, didn't he?"

"He didn't have to use that knife."

"Well, he used it."

"And look where it's got us," complained Dorris. "We've got to lie low for a coupla months, and we haven't got the dough to do it on."

Marriott gave a sudden flash of a grin.

"Might have to work!"

"Don't talk to me about work." Dorris grinned too.

In their way, these men were good friends. They had been to school together, and had left at the age of fifteen. They had gone to work in the docks together. While Dorris had boxed, Marriott had led a small, squalid, rather brutal and not very effective gang. Dorris had joined the gang, later, and by brute strength cowed all the others into accepting Marriott's leadership. It was a fact that he still regarded Marriott as the "brains" of any outfit they belonged to. They had migrated to crime easily, at first restricting activities to pilfering from the docks, then becoming bolder and carrying out one or two raids on isolated shops in London suburbs, gradually aiming higher, dreaming of one big deal which would see them in clover for months. They had talked and dreamed of it, and this deal today should have been the one.

Five thousand pounds was the kind of target they regarded as really big.

But they had needed a getaway car, or lorry, and so a driver. They had also needed someone to look after any guard who was around.

Alec Gool was a young cousin of Marriott, and Gool had introduced Steve Stevens to them.

Since they had divided the proceeds of the robbery, they had not met the other two.

Marriott would not admit it in so many words, but he was uneasy about Stevens. He did not like Gool, who was a lot too big for his boots, but thought of the youth as a kid who could easily be handled. Stevens wasn't a kid. There was something about the way he looked at you—

There was something about the way Steve looked at her, Joyce Conway thought. She did not quite understand it. She had seen naked desire and lust in many a man's eyes, and knew what it meant and how to deal with any situation that it created. She knew how to handle maudlin drunks, women-hungry sailors, sex-starved men who had been in prison for years. These people she knew all about, and in a way could feel sorry for them. She was not surprised and certainly not shocked that a lot of girls and some women of her own age were content to satisfy these men, sometimes for love, sometimes for the physical thrill, more often for money or a good time, but she wasn't having anything to do with that kind of thing.

She had always kept her self-respect; she governed her life by the need for it.

It had been difficult, since Tom had died twelve years ago. Twelve *years*. Sometimes, in fact whenever she thought of it, she found that hard to believe, it seemed at once so long and yet so short a time. Occasionally she would try to picture what he would look like today, if he were alive. In a funny way, she thought he might look like Steve, but with a difference. He'd had the same lean kind of face and features as Steve, even his eyes had been the same pale grey, but in a way those eyes of his had always caressed her.

There was nothing gentle about Steve.

There was the difference, of course; Tom had been a gentle, kindly man, almost too soft-hearted. Steve was hard and unyielding. Tom had never really known what he wanted – in fact he had not wanted anything more than his little home and his family and a job – whereas Steve knew exactly what he was after, and meant to get it. She sensed that. He was a handsome eagle of a man, she could imagine that when the right moment came he would swoop on his victim without mercy. And yet something about him fascinated her; something about the way he looked at her, as if he were saying:

"I'm waiting for you. You won't escape me."

Perhaps, she told herself, she was making it up. Perhaps he didn't think much about her. At least he didn't seem to have much to do with the whores, or any of the girls who flung themselves at the heads of the sailors who had come fresh from a voyage with their pockets lined. Stevens was aloof; different; and it was that difference which attracted her.

Joyce had been barmaid at the Hornpipe for eight of the years of her widowhood. That was how she came to know so many men, and what the girls were like, which women were faithful to lovers or to husbands, and which would flit around men like drunks round the bar. Over the years she had won a respect which no one really challenged these days – it must be a year since anyone had even tried to get fresh with her. Except at Christmas, of course, there was always a bit of kissing and cuddling at Christmas, and it often stirred a memory of desire, but she soon forgot it again. A single bed was only lonely if one missed one's man.

She was thirty-seven.

Both her children had been born before she was twenty. Richard was now in Australia. He had gone on a merchant ship and got off in Sydney and stayed there. Now and again he sent her a little present and now and again wrote a scratchy airmail letter, but she had a feeling that he would never come home. Jennifer was married, had two children of her own, and lived out at Harlow New Town.

When she had first gone to live there, close to her husband's job, she had come in to London once a week regularly, but now it was once a month, and a third baby was on the way.

Joyce Conway didn't mind.

She was free of the responsibilities, after doing all a widowed woman could for her children. You couldn't make children good or bad, of course – she had seen too many try – and she had been lucky. Jennifer was a good girl, and always would be. Richard was a bit wild, she couldn't imagine him sticking to one woman for long, but he would do no one any harm intentionally. In any case, Joyce now had only herself to worry about.

The first man to make her think *of* a man for a long time, was Steve Stevens.

It was a year since he had first come into the Hornpipe with two other sailors, standing head-and-shoulders above them in height and appearance. Apart from his lean good looks, he was clean-shaven – freshly shaven, too. He wore a good suit, and it fitted perfectly. He had manners, usually. True, his eyes had dropped to her plunge line pretty quickly – Jack Harris, the boss, liked the barmaids to attract the male eye, it made sure of custom – but Stevens hadn't made any cracks, and hadn't leered. She remembered that for a few nights after he had been in she had half expected him, and glanced up whenever she had time and the door opened; but he hadn't come for two weeks. By then, she had stopped looking.

After his seventh or eighth visit, he had asked her to go to a matinée in the West End with him.

The curious thing was that he hadn't asked the obvious questions, hadn't said much at all. They had been to matinées several times since, he'd bought her chocolates, been the proper gentleman, and yet there was something about the way he looked at her – on the bus, in the taxi he sometimes sported, in the restaurant after the Hornpipe was closed and she could relax. She knew that he had learned nearly everything about her, she talked so much out of the depth of her loneliness; but apart from the fact that he was a merchant seaman who worked as little as he could, she knew little about him. She knew he had once been in the Royal Navy, he had let out the fact that he had been in some minor action in the Far East, China or somewhere; but that was all. He lodged with a family in Dick Street, near the main docks.

He didn't come in for a drink every night, but she always looked out for him, now.

Tonight – the night of the murder of Charley Blake and the terrible injuries of Paul Bennison – she wondered if he would come. It was nine o'clock, and much quieter than usual. Three big ships had sailed on the afternoon tide, and a storm in the Atlantic had delayed others from arriving. So she was able to keep glancing at the *Evening News,* which she kept on the shelf beneath the bar. The shiny wooden handles of the taps were on her right and left, and she could serve mild and bitter, stout, dark, any one of eight varieties of beer almost without looking at the handles themselves. She could take any one of the usual spirits off the shelves behind her almost by habit, too. She had grown so accustomed to the sour odour of beer and the sharper one of the spirits, the thick tobacco smoke, the curious salty, tangy, sweaty stink of so many of the men, that she hardly noticed them.

The headlines ran:

WAGES GUARD DEAD
CASHIER BADLY WOUNDED

There hadn't been much more news that day, so this was still the main story. There were photographs: a bad one of the dead man, a good one of the family of the injured man. She looked at the face of Mrs Bennison and the smiling children and thought mechanically: *What a shame.* One of the boys was a bit like Richard. There was a photograph of Bennison, too, and he reminded her of a film star, who was it? Gregory Peck, that was the one – he wasn't really like Greg, but there was a likeness especially about the forehead and eyes. *What a shame.*

"Learning to squint?" Steve asked, his voice very close to her.

She started, looked up, laughed, and said: "Steve! I didn't see you coming in."

"You weren't looking. What's so exciting?"

"Only another of those wage snatches," said Joyce. "What are you going to have?"

"On the house?"

"Not likely."

"Whisky-and-soda," said Steve. "A double."

"Getting your strength up?"

"What would I need strength for?" demanded Steve. He smiled at her, and she laughed, just a little uneasy and a little excited, then turned round for the whisky. In the decorated mirror behind the bar she could see him, and when she turned round, with the whisky in the small glass, she saw that his gaze rested on her bosom – he had stared like that more lately than in the past. She put the whisky down, and put a larger glass with some ice cubes in front of him; he liked his whisky on the rocks, American style, although he had never said that he had been to the United States.

"Have one with me," he invited.

"No, Steve, ta."

"Don't you ever relax?"

"If I started drinking behind the bar I'd get fat."

"Fat *and* a squint," he jeered. He raised his glass. "*Prosit.*" He often uttered a toast in a foreign language, but *prosit* and *skol* were his favourites. He looked into her eyes as he drank, and she had the impression that he was more eager than usual for the drink. "Hungry?" he asked.

"I might be, in an hour's time."

"That's a date."

"All right, Steve, but—" she broke off.

"But what?"

"You don't *have* to buy my supper every time you come in."

"I wouldn't buy anyone anything I had to," he said. "There's something I want to know, though."

"What's that?"

"Are you a good cook?"

The two street doors opened at the same time, and there was an influx of visitors. Joyce did not recognise all of them, for they were sailors off a ship which must have come in during the afternoon; Dutchmen, she could tell that from their cigars and something about their heavy jowls. From the other side of the bar came a youth she didn't like – although occasionally he was with Steve. He was Alec Gool. She had known him ever since his childhood – in fact he had gone to school with Richard, and at one time Richard had started running the streets with him. Then Richard had fallen off a bicycle and broken his leg, and by the time he was about again, the gang of young hooligans had run off. There was something funny about Alec Gool, and always had been; he was cat-like. There were rumours that he was a queer, too – that he never went with girls.

He stood just inside the room, looking about him, clean-cut features, rather on the short side for a man, his fair hair beautifully waved, as if he had come from a hairdresser, although she knew his hair was like that, as natural as it could be, since he had been a child. He saw Steve, but didn't move towards him. He went to the other end of the bar, where Jack Harris was in charge.

Then the Dutchmen gave their orders in deep, harsh English, and she was busy – too busy even to think much about Steve's cryptic question: was she a good cook? She knew what he meant, of course; he wanted her to cook a meal for him. She knew Steve, or she thought she did, better than she knew most men. He had a habit of saying a lot in a short, terse sentence. *Are you a good cook?* As she poured out rum, whisky and schnapps for the lively Dutchmen, Steve stood a little to one side, watching her. His lips were curved as he smiled – he seldom smiled enough to show his teeth. His eyes were half laughing, too, and their expression was different from any she had seen in them before.

He meant: *"I want to come home with you."* He probably meant: *"I want to come home and sleep with you."* Or was that her imagination? Was she putting words into his mouth? She wished she really did understand him.

The rush was over as suddenly as it began.

"Well, are you?" Steve asked.

"I have been a good cook, in my time," she said. "I don't get much practice these days."

"That's what I want to put right," he said. "You shouldn't leave anything alone too long. You forget how good it is."

That had a double meaning, surely she couldn't be mistaken? She forced herself to laugh, and then another influx of sailors and stevedores arrived, and for ten minutes she was pulling the beer handles and opening bottles with the unflurried speed which made her so good at her job. Steve moved away from the bar. When she saw him next, he was sitting by the window, opposite Alec Gool. They were talking, and Gool seemed to be very earnest. Now and again, Steve shook his head. Suddenly, he finished his drink and stood up. Gool did the same. Without a glance round, without the slightest hint of a glance, they went out.

When the door closed, it was as if he had shut her out of his life.

Joyce was surprised, then hurt, then annoyed. She should have been used to that kind of departure by now. He would do whatever he wanted, and would not be deterred by her or anyone else. She hadn't exactly encouraged him to stop, either. No one less like Tom could be imagined, and yet—

Why had he gone out with Gool? Was Gool a *queer?*

And what about Steve? There was a lot of talk about sailors, especially sailors who were at sea for a long time without the release of a visit to port. She didn't really know what to think, and before she closed the door behind her, just after a quarter to eleven, when she was finished at the pub, she told herself that she was wasting her time by giving him a second thought.

But she wished she knew what he and Alec Gool were up to.

Chapter Seven

Threat

"… so I think we ought to do another snatch, quick. Then we can lie low for a few weeks," Marriott said.

Now, all four of them were together. They were in a corner of a bowling rink, which was used by seamen, dock labourers, stevedores, and casual workers. No liquor was being served, because it was after hours, but there was coffee in front of Marriott and Dorris, and a lemonade in front of Alec Gool. Steve was smoking, not drinking.

"It stands to reason," Dorris said.

Neither Gool nor Steve spoke.

"I know the very place—" Marriott began. "They draw the dough on Saturdays, they think that will fool us, but—"

"You knew the very place this morning," Steve said, coldly.

"Well, there was some dough, wasn't there?"

"Remember you promised us five thousand?"

"I couldn't help it if a lying son of a bitch told me it was five thou', could I?" protested Marriott. He was uneasy about Stevens.

"Where is this chap now?" Stevens asked.

"Which chap?"

"Your so-called informant? Can he do us any harm?"

"He's okay, he wouldn't ever—"

"Let's have it," Stevens said in a hard voice. "Who is he? When he hears about what happened today will he put a finger on you?"

"No!"

"What makes you so sure?"

"I tell you he won't! We can trust him, even if he puts two and two together."

"If you don't tell me who he is you'll have to put yourself together, I'll tear you into little pieces." Stevens's voice was low-pitched and hard. "Come on—who was he?"

"You've got no right—"

Stevens put his hand to his waist and pulled at the handle of his knife until half-an-inch of the blade showed; glistening. Marriott stared at it, then into Stevens's eyes.

"Let's have it," Stevens said. "Who was he?"

Marriott muttered: "I—I heard a couple of bank guards talking. They – they said he came every Friday and collected five, I—I thought they meant thousands. They didn't know I was listening."

Into a tense silence, Stevens said: "So that's what we took these risks for. You ought to have your tongue cut out." The glint in his eyes matched that of the knife, blade, and the tension seemed to reach breaking point.

Dorris broke it, nervously.

"Anyone can make a mistake, Steve."

"That's right," Stevens said. "But only a fool makes the same one twice. We were seen by too many people this morning. We stay away from banks and post offices until the trouble's blown over. And if you think you know better than me, go and jump in the river. We're not doing another snatch until this one's been forgotten."

"Who the hell do you think you're talking to?" Marriott began to bluster, and a girl at the next table looked round. "If it hadn't been for you—"

Stevens's right hand moved. Something sharp jabbed into Marriott's leg, and he winced, and pushed his chair back. Steve was staring at him fixedly – and Steve's right hand was out of sight, under the table. Marriott could feel the blood beginning to ooze out of a little stab wound, and he knew exactly what had happened. He thought, fearfully, that Steve was too ready with his knife, that it was dangerous to work with him.

"Don't make any mistakes," Stevens said. "We're going to have a rest."

Dorris was looking at Marriott, for a lead.

"If either of you start anything you'll have me to answer to, as well as the police," Stevens went on. His voice only just carried to the two men, and to Alec. "That clear?"

Marriott licked his lips.

"Maybe that's the way I want it, too, but—"

"Let's go, Alec," Steve said. He stood up, then leaned on the table and kept his voice very low, but both Marriott and Dorris could hear. "We don't want to be seen together for a few weeks, the cops know that four men were in this morning's job, and they'll know what kind of an assortment it was. You keep to yourself and keep out of trouble. Otherwise—"

He didn't finish.

When the door had closed on him and Alec, Marriott glared into Dorris's eyes, and asked harshly: "Who does he think he is?"

"Win—"

"I'll teach him, before he's much older," Marriott went on savagely. He was angry and pale-faced, but had the sense to keep his voice low. "One of these days—"

"Want me to do him?" asked Dorris. He clenched his hands on top of the table.

"Not yet," said Marriott. "The time will come. Who the hell does he think he is?"

Steve Stevens and Alec walked along the narrow road, from the club, Stevens's strides long and easy, Alec making an effort to keep pace. They passed beneath a gas lamp, and Alec glanced up and saw the way the other's lips were set, saw how his jaw was thrust forward. Steve was staring straight ahead. Two policemen passed the end of the street, but did not even glance down it, as far as the men could judge.

"Steve."

"What?"

"Those two can be dangerous."

"I know who can be dangerous."

"Know what I think?"

Steve glanced down. "Yes, I know what you think. But it doesn't make you right."

"What do I think?"

Steve did not answer at once. They reached the corner, and he looked across at another, where the Hornpipe was in darkness but for a light at a top floor window, in Harris and his wife's bedroom. Shadows moved against the curtains. The only sound was an aeroplane, droning up high, and distant noises at the docks. To the south, the sky was lighted up by the great lights which played on the ships which were being worked by night, ready for the morning tide. The two men turned left.

"I asked you a question," Alec said.

Steve still didn't respond. He knew that if anyone else had talked to him like that he would have slapped their mouths so hard that they would not have been able to talk with comfort for a week. He could take things from Alec which he wouldn't take from anyone else. There were just two people for whom he had any feeling and with whom he had any patience; one was this youth of eighteen, the other was Joyce Conway. Joyce lived in one of the nearby tiny terraced houses, drab grey grimy places which had survived London's blitzes and the work of the slum clearance Acts. She had the ground floor, sleeping in the front room and living in the back. Upstairs was let to a middle-aged couple and one unmarried daughter.

"Something on your mind?" Alec asked.

"You think that we ought to put those two away," said Steve, "and you could be right—later. But not yet. Too many people have seen all of us together. They're too scared to do anything much yet, but—watch them, Alec. Make sure they don't try to do another job. If they do a job and get caught they might start talking."

"You've got round to it," Alec said, half sneering.

"What's that?"

"You've got round to seeing why they ought to be—"

"Alec," Steve interrupted, "don't make me lose my temper. Just watch them. They're too scared to take any chances just now, and they still have a hundred quid or more each, to last them for a week or two. We can decide what to do with them later, but we don't do anything yet. Got that?"

"You're the boss."

"Remember it."

"Bosses can be wrong," Alec observed.

They reached a long, narrow street of tiny terraced houses, where they both lived. Alec turned to the doorway of his house, which was in darkness, but a street lamp was just opposite it, and the light reflected on the window. He paused only for a fraction of a second:

"G'night."

"'Night," Steve said.

He did not miss a step, but walked with his long, raking impatient stride towards the far end of the street, where he lodged. He had a front room, and was looked after well. He kept the room on even when he was at sea. These days he spent less time at sea. He was tired of wandering, tired of having no settled home, tired of taking his women where he found them. He knew all this. He had a clear mind and a sound intelligence, and also knew that he had one all-consuming weakness: that of giving way to impulse. It had got him into most of the troubles of his active life.

Before today, he had killed twice. Once it had been in a brawl over a woman in a South American port during a voyage on a stinking cargo ship. He could picture her dark-haired snaky beauty now, the way her body had writhed and twisted in a kind of seductive frenzy; and he could remember her tall, elderly husband – his first victim.

The second brawl had been in an Australian port, when a drunken sot had accused him of fixing his cards, at poker.

Stevens did not fix cards.

He knew much of the world. He knew the torment of weeks at sea, in hot, breathless days with a steamer chugging on its seemingly endless voyage. He knew the icy blast of arctic winters, when the sea seemed made of ice. He could remember most things that had happened to him since his childhood, but he could never recall much about that. A drunken kindly father, often at sea. A pretty, fluffy mother who had a lot of men friends—

His impulses were not always simply flares of temper. It had been on impulse, for instance, that he had worked with the others today. He was short of money. Alec had told him what was being planned, and sold him the idea that the job would be worth five thousand pounds. When he had met Marriott and Dorris he had not liked them, but they had seemed tough enough – and they had proved tough enough.

So had he.

Now he realised that he should never have done it. He should never have left the planning to Marriott. That had been due to his other besetting weakness – laziness. If a thing could be done for him, he preferred that to doing it for himself. It had been too much trouble to plan his own job, and now he was at the mercy of Marriott and Dorris. He could not be sure that he judged them aright, but on balance he believed that they would do he had told them. He was a little uneasy about Dorris, not sure that the ex-boxer had been as cowed as Marriott.

None of this would have been so bad if he had come away with a fair amount of money, but a hundred and thirty-three pounds!

It was laughable.

He hesitated outside the front door of the house where he lodged, but knew that he was not going straight in. It was a quarter past eleven, early yet, too early to he in bed and read, or listen to the radio, or put on some records. He would not be able to relax. He had never felt right, after killing. It seemed to release some pent-up store of energy in him; he had to have an outlet for it before he could rest. Now, he was as wide awake as he had ever been.

He walked on, to Joyce's place.

His mood kindled at the thought of Joyce. He wondered if she knew the effect she had on him – an effect which had been instantaneous. He could remember opening the door of the Hornpipe, stepping in, looking across the fog of blue-grey smoke, and seeing her. He doubted if she knew what she looked like. In the East End, among all the riff-raff, a real jewel could easily be overlooked because there were so many glittering imitations. All his life he had liked mature women, and this one had a curious look of maturity and also of purity. Virginity, rather. She had the look of a young girl. He had never put it into words, but in fact he sensed that she had a quality of goodness. The word itself would have made him laugh derisively, for goodness, to him, meant weakness and prosiness and smoothness. But virginity – that was something he could understand. Joyce had a complexion you didn't often see outside of Italy, Spain or the South of France. Now and again you would see a young London Jewess with it, but few women in their middle-thirties retained it. And she had hazel-brown eyes, very clear, not even slightly bloodshot, made up with only a very slight touch of eyeshade. She had the sense to know that her complexion gave her eyes all the brightness they needed. She laughed so easily; happily. That was another thing he realised about her, she was a happy person.

Everyone liked her – even young Alec Gool, who had no time for women, respected her. Stevens had first learnt about her years of widowhood, about her daughter with the children and her son in Australia, from Alec. The East End was like a country village, everyone knew all there was to know about his neighbour – or thought he did.

The odd thing was that Joyce's dark hair was turning grey at the temples and with a few streaks where she drew it back from the forehead, and instead of making her look older, it made her look younger. He had noticed the way she dealt with the customers, especially the drunks, and she had soothed him.

She always did. He liked being with her. He had wanted to spend not only the evening but the night with her. It would not be long before he did, but – he was anxious that she should want him. He was in love with her, of course, but whenever he realised this, he reacted against it – being in love implied dependence on her, and he would be dependent on no one.

He reached her house; and the light was on in the front room, her bedroom. He could see it at the edges of the curtains and at the tiny gap in the middle.

He thought of her, in bed.

Oh God, he wanted her!

He went close to the window, which was flush with the pavement, and tapped. There was no response. He tapped again, a little rhythm that always amused her, from: *What shall we do with a drunken sailor? Da-di-di-da-di-da-di-da-da-da!* Out here in the street, the tap of his knuckles on the glass sounded quite loud, but there was still no response. She *must* know he was there. She wasn't going to pretend that she didn't, was she? He clenched his fist, and drew it back, to make more noise, but just managed to stop himself. He gritted his teeth. There was a pain at the back of his head from a headache which he had kept at bay all day. If he let himself go he would smash that window. If he –

The door opened, and light shone out.

"Steve, what are you doing there?"

She was framed in the doorway, still fully dressed, but her hair was down to her shoulders. It was like a halo, misty against the dim light behind her. He could not see her face clearly. He felt the anger ease out of his body, taking tension with it.

"I want to see you," he said. "I didn't think I would be so long. I was going to buy you supper, remember?"

Wasn't she going to ask him in?

"I haven't had mine yet," she said quietly. "But it's too late to go to a restaurant." She drew back into the narrow passage. "You'd better come in."

He stepped past her. She closed the door. They were very close to each other, the passage so narrow that his back was touching one wall, hers must be touching the other. He was a head taller. He could go along the passage into the bedroom, or further along, into the living room and kitchen – he had been here, twice, briefly. He felt an all-consuming desire for her. He did not move away, but slid his arms round her and brought her very close, pressing himself against her.

"Joyce, tonight's the night," he said roughly. "It's got to be tonight." He held her so that her head was back, her lips were parted a little, glistening. He crushed them with his own. He kissed her cheeks, her nose, her eyes, her throat. "Joyce, tonight's the night, it's got to be tonight."

Joyce had never intended it to be like this, but as she heard his hoarse voice and felt the pressure of his Ups, his hands, his arms, his body, she had a sense of his great need.

Chapter Eight

Second Visit

Roger West reached his home in Bell Street, Chelsea, a little after seven o'clock that night. He knew that his two sons, Martin-called-Scoop and Richard-sometimes-called-Fish, would not be home. They had gone for a long weekend to a camp organised by their school. In a way, he was glad. He felt tired and on edge, and it would be difficult to be patient with youthful high spirits, if the need for patience arose.

He put the car into the garage, and recalled how very like the Bennisons' garage it was, then walked along the crazy paving path to the back door. He heard music on; Janet probably hadn't heard him. He went in by the back door, where the sound of music was louder. Janet wasn't in here, but the kitchen was spick-and-span, as always. The oven light glowed, so she had something cooking for him. His eyes and his thoughts kindled.

He went along the passage leading from the kitchen to the front room, peered in, but Janet wasn't there, either. His chair was drawn up closer to the window, the morning and evening newspapers, cigarettes, whisky and soda were on a small table by the side of the chair; whenever he was late, Janet got these things ready. The radio was on in the room.

Where was she?

He smiled to himself, and went upstairs, all the sound he made muffled by the music. Then he saw her – in their bedroom, which overlooked Bell Street. She was looking at herself in the dressing table mirror, which was so placed that she couldn't see the reflection of anyone in the doorway. She was peering forward, lips pursed, and slowly put her head on one side. She had a pink towel round her shoulders, and her blouse was lying on the foot of the double bed. She turned her head round slightly in the other direction. Roger crept towards her. Any moment she might turn and see him, but she was so intent on her self-appraisal that she didn't notice. He stretched forward, touched the towel and snatched it off her shoulders.

She jumped wildly.

"Roger!"

In pulling the towel, he also pulled off one of the thin shoulder straps of her brassiere. Her shoulders were bare, it was easy to see the depth of her bosom, and the satiny smoothness of her skin. As she turned round, face uplifted, eyes bright although partly because he had scared her, head tilted back, she looked – wonderful. She had looked wonderful for over twenty years. He leaned down and kissed her with more passion than he had for a long time. When he drew back, she was a little breathless.

"Hallo, my darling," Roger said.

"I love you," said Janet, in a rather husky voice. "Why did you do that?"

"Kiss you?"

"Kiss me like that?"

"You looked so desirable."

"Seriously."

"I'm serious," he assured her. "You look—"

"You couldn't see me."

"I could see enough of you," he retorted, and glanced at the drooping brassiere.

She smiled, but he sensed that she was still thoughtful.

"Roger, did you know?"

"Know what?"

"What I've been doing?"

"No," he said. "If you've been doing anything unusual, or anything you shouldn't, I've been completely unaware. No detective knows anything about his wife and family. What *have* you been up to?"

"Just for a moment I thought you knew," said Janet, looking a little wistful. "I've been using a new skin cream for two or three weeks. I think it *has* made a difference—it's given me a—" she broke off, and her eyes seemed to tease as well as to laugh. "Well, what *has* it given me?"

Roger studied her closely, and began to realise that she had in fact looked at her best lately; perhaps a little younger. He should have told her so, but hadn't thought to. Now he studied her closely, using his training in observation to pick out the difference – and suddenly he saw and understood.

"Really want to know?" he asked.

"Go on. Guess!"

"It's no guess, it's certain knowledge. It's given you a kind of bloom."

Her eyes lit up.

"Do you really think so? That's exactly what it's supposed to do, and it isn't expensive—the chemist makes it up, ten shillings' worth will last three months. Roger, it *is* worth it, isn't it?"

"It's cheap at the price."

"I'd just been brushing my hair, and I thought my skin was better," Janet said. She stood up, quickly. "You must be famished. I've a chop and some vegetables in the oven, it won't be two jiffs." She hooked the narrow strap back over her shoulder, dodged his roaming hand, and slid into the green shirt blouse. "I do *not* want any help in doing it up," she said, slapping his hand away. "What kind of a day have you had, darling?"

Until that moment, and for five minutes, he had forgotten. Recollection came over him like a dark shadow. He said: "So-so," and followed her out of the room and down the stairs. At the foot, she turned to look at him thoughtfully, and when they were in the kitchen, and he was sipping a whisky and soda while watching her get his supper out of the oven, she said: "It's been rough, has it?"

"Pretty rough."

"That Covent Garden murder?"

"Yes."

"That poor woman," Janet said. Her face was flushed from the heat of the oven as she brought the steaming, piled-up plate out, topped with an aluminium saucepan lid. "How is the man Bennison? The evening paper says he's critically ill."

"They're certainly right," Roger said. He tossed down the rest of the whisky. "Very critically ill."

Janet didn't respond, but fetched salt and pepper, bread and butter, a big dish with a little fruit jelly left in it, and put all these on the table.

"Let it cool down for a few minutes," she advised.

He wished that she had not changed the subject so abruptly; this was one of the evenings when he would like to talk to her; talking so often helped. He wanted to get his mind completely clear on the case, and Janet knew almost as well as he did himself that he would have little rest from it tonight.

"I think I'll have another tot," he said.

"I'll get it."

"No, I—"

She smiled into his face, very soberly. She was nice-looking, dark, not even slightly matronly. And at this moment she was very serious.

"Sit down, darling," she said. "I'll get you another drink. Do you want to wash?"

He washed his hands and face at the kitchen sink, and when she came back, he was draping his jacket over the back of a chair.

"Thanks." He sipped.

"Have you seen Mrs Bennison?"

"Yes."

"I had a feeling that you had," said Janet. "I wondered if it was one of those cases."

"*Those?*" She often startled him with this kind of comment.

"The cases that affect you emotionally," Janet said, carefully. "They're so much harder to solve, aren't they? Do you think you know who did it?"

"Not yet," said Roger. After a pause, he went on: "We've descriptions of three men involved, but they might fit a lot of people. We didn't find a single finger-print or foot-print that was of any use. Three men in the lab have been going through everything we swept up from the spot where it happened—and haven't found a thing. Hundreds of people go past there every hour. No one who saw the men recognised them – they were strangers to the market … "

He hardly realised how rapidly he was talking, or how intent Janet was.

"… We thought at first that it might have been an attack on the wrong man, as only five hundred pounds was involved, but I think the indications are it was meant for Bennison. They must have seen him often before, if they watched Revel's. The attack on the guard came later – and after he came face to face with his killer. That could indicate that guard and killer knew each other. I'm trying to get someone in the vicinity to remember if they've seen anyone resembling the attackers before, but no luck so far. Some people who saw the men leaving the lorry in Goswell Road have described two of the men pretty clearly, and the descriptions tally with those of the eye-witnesses to the actual attack, but even that doesn't get us much further. Whenever we pick up suspects we should be able to get the men picked out in an identification parade but first we want those men. All the Divisions are busy, and we've had sketches made of the images that the eye-witnesses were able to give us, but that doesn't always do much good. I've got an uneasy feeling about the case."

He stopped, at last.

"Darling," Janet said, "when you get emotionally involved you always have an uneasy feeling. I shouldn't worry too much about that. What's made you feel guilty?"

"Don't be silly, I don't feel guilty!"

"Don't you?"

He looked at her, a little put out at first, then suddenly he laughed. He finished the drink, and sat down in front of the food heaped up on his plate. The aroma from it, the moment the saucepan lid was off, was enough to make him feel ravenous.

"A silly thing," he said. "She asked me why I—why we let these things happen."

He began to eat. Janet didn't speak, but went and sat on the other side of the kitchen table, with its pale green formica top, and the steam from the meal misted her features slightly.

"I suppose, when you're worked up like that, you'll say anything," Janet said. After a pause, she went on: "Were you able to help her?"

"Not much," Roger said. "Jan—" he hesitated, then pushed his chair back. "There's a risk that it will turn Bennison into an idiot."

Janet caught her breath.

"So the surgeon says," said Roger, savagely. "There's no certainty but—" he broke off, pulled his chair up again, and began to eat with less appetite. "If I could only get one single clue I would feel better, but it's a complete blank. What we really depend on is luck. I know we often do, but usually we have something that will point the way. This time, we haven't."

"What kind of luck do you need?"

"We want someone who saw the men today to catch sight of them again," Roger said. "Oh, we'll work on the descriptions, but I'm not really sanguine."

"That could be because you've taken it so hard," Janet said.

"Could be." Roger left some potatoes and some runner beans on his plate, but finished the rich, meaty chop. "That was good! What—hey! What are you having?" His voice rose, and he was annoyed with himself for being so preoccupied that he hadn't noticed until now that Janet wasn't eating.

"I had a big tea over at May Hargreaves," Janet said. "All I need is a snack later. Where do the Bennisons five?"

"Wimbledon," Roger answered absently.

"I've been in nearly all day," said Janet. "And we haven't had a drive across Wimbledon Common for months. Would you like to go for a run, and look in?"

She realised just how much the Bennison family was on his mind, of course.

"It might be a good idea," he agreed.

"I'll get my hat," Janet said. "Let's say ten minutes."

They were at the Bennisons just before a quarter to nine. Half-a-dozen people were in the street, and a policeman was on duty, obviously to clear the crowd along. When the car drew up, a girl appeared at the front door of the house, tall, grave-faced, not at all like her mother – for this was Rose Bennison. She looked puzzled when she saw Roger, as if she half recognised him.

"I'm awfully sorry," she said formally, "but my mother isn't able to see anyone. She—"

"I'm Superintendent West," Roger explained. "My wife and I were passing, and we thought ..."

The girl's eyes lit up.

Indoors, eight-year-old Michael Bennison was already in bed and asleep. A grave-faced Paul Junior was sitting at a table in the living room, with text books in front of him. Mrs Bennison had some mending by her side. She jumped up quickly as Roger and Janet entered. "Rose, you should have told me!" She moved her chair back and pushed the mending-box on to a bookcase shelf by the chair, momentarily confused. "Paul dear, this is Superintendent West, the man who—"

She broke off.

"I know who he is," Paul said. He stood up from the table, but made no attempt to come forward. Roger, thinking more of the mother than of the children, moved across with his hand outstretched. The first indication that all was not well came when Paul hesitated for a long time before taking his hand; then the boy simply touched it, and withdrew quickly. Roger saw that he was more than grave; he was stony-faced. There was no light at all in his eyes, which were grey and had become slate grey.

He stared at Roger unwinkingly.

"I'm so very sorry," Janet was saying to Mrs Bennison.

Roger thought: I've two sons of my own, much about the age of this boy, yet I don't know how to talk to him. He wanted to say something to break down the barrier which had been built, unseen, on that moment of meeting, but at all costs he must not say the wrong thing.

"I talked to the surgeon who operated on your father," he said at last. "He is a brilliant man."

After a pause, the boy said flatly: "Is he?"

"Rose, put a kettle on and make some coffee, will you? Paul, pop over to Mrs Abbott and say that I'll be over later." Mrs Bennison was trying desperately to keep the situation from getting out of hand, fighting for normality – her sewing, the boy's work, the instant decision to make coffee. Her tension and nervousness showed in the way her hands trembled, touching first a button on her navy-blue cardigan, then her hair, then her wedding ring.

"All right, Mum," the girl said.

The boy hesitated, stared again at Roger, and went out. He was very tall for a lad of twelve, and moved well; rather like Richard, at home.

"Do come into the other room," said Mrs Bennison. She led the way, and hesitated at the door of the front room, caught between going in first, and standing aside for them. As a result, she collided, breast to breast, with Roger. Her body was stiff, her bosom firm. "I'm sorry," she said, and wasn't far from tears. Yet in a way that helped, because she gave a little sniff and a choked sob, and stepped ahead hurriedly. Her voice was stronger. "Do sit down. It was very nice of you to call. Michael will be all right, and so will Rose, but— well, Paul's the one who worries me. He hasn't said a word since he was told what happened. Not a word. He just got out the books for his holiday task and started reading. It's almost as if he's pretending that it didn't happen."

Then she switched the subject quickly. "Mr West, have you any fresh news? Mr Semple-Smith, the surgeon, told me that it will be five or six days before we can be sure that my husband is out of danger. Nothing's changed, has it?"

As she spoke, a hideous thought obviously occurred to her, and for a moment she went so pale that Roger thought she was going to faint. "Paul's not—"

"Nothing's changed at all," Roger said hurriedly. "I really came to tell you that you can be absolutely sure that the best possible advice will be available for your husband—everything humanly possible will be done to help him."

Mrs Bennison dropped on to the edge of a chair, and put one unsteady hand in front of her face.

"Thank you," she said. "Thank you very much."

"And we want to know if there is anything we can do to help you," Roger went on after a pause.

"No," she said, huskily. "No, I shall be all right. Mr Revel has been in, he is very good. I shall be all right. I'm worried about Paul, but it's early yet."

Everyone was very good, Isobel Bennison thought when the Wests had gone. Everyone. But nothing altered the fact that in a few moments their whole life had been savagely attacked. Nothing altered the fact that Paul lay in that hospital bed, drugged, desperately ill, with his broken body, perhaps dying, perhaps dead. Oh, God. It was so lonely. Rose tried to help but she was so young as well as frightened; while Paul was – strange.

She hardly recognised her own son.

Later, in bed, alone, she began to cry. In the next room Rose lay sleeping, but across the landing Paul lay awake, listening, hearing.

"I know exactly how you must feel," Janet said to Roger. "I want results as desperately as you do. That boy looked almost like an old man."

There was no news, and no clue, on the Saturday, and none on Sunday.

On Monday and Tuesday the Divisional chiefs reported one after another that they had not been able to put their hands on any one who answered the description of the robbers and who had suddenly come into money. With the exception of the man who had actually knifed Charley Blake, the descriptions of the others were so general that they might have fitted any one of hundreds of people.

"No one with a record of wages snatches or hold-ups of any kind fits in," the Divisional men all told Roger.

"The truth is that they didn't get away with enough cash to make them start painting the town red," said one. "There's one thing I am doing, though."

"What's that?" asked Roger, forcing an interest. "I'm checking all the boxing men on the fringe of this kind of job," the South Eastern Superintendent told him. "According to a further statement from two of the witnesses, one of the men had a cauliflower ear." "Get after them," Roger said.

When he rang off, he faced the fact that he had a sense almost of defeatism; only one thing could counter that effectively. He looked across at Cope, said: "Ask Simpson to meet me at Revel's office in an hour's time," and went downstairs and got into his car. This time he drove himself. Driving in the thick traffic absorbed him enough to ease the sense of failure. He drove first to Charing Cross Hospital, took a chance with parking, and went to inquire about Bennison. A Yard man was by Bennison's bedside all the time, in case the victim should come round and make some comment; or in case he talked in his drugged sleep. As Roger turned into the passage, the ward door opened and Mrs Bennison came out, followed by a nurse. They stopped.

"Good morning," Roger said. "How is he?" "Just the same," replied Mrs Bennison. "I didn't realise you had a man with him all the time." "My man wasn't in the way, was he?" "No. I just didn't realise it."

"Can I drive you anywhere?"

"No," Mrs Bennison said, and then changed her mind: "Well, I wonder if you're going anywhere near—Paul's office."

"In five minutes," Roger said. "I won't be a minute longer."

In fact he spent less time than that with elderly, white-haired Detective Sergeant Winfrith, who sat with a book in his hand and a notebook and pencil handy. Winfrith was a gentle-voiced man who had broken an ankle chasing thieves over a rooftop, a few years ago, and was given as many sedentary jobs as the Yard could find for him.

"He hasn't stirred, sir," he reported.

Roger nodded. "So I gather." He looked over the top of a screen at the face of the unconscious man, and had a shock for the face was so like young Paul's. It also looked like the face of death beneath that turban of bandages.

He went out, understanding even more of Isobel Bennison's frame of mind.

She got into the car and he took the wheel.

"How is young Paul?" he asked.

"He hardly says a word," Isobel Bennison replied. "I honestly don't know what to do with him."

"Have you had a word with his doctor?"

"I haven't yet. I suppose I should." Roger was keenly aware of her intentness. "I feel so helpless," she went on. "I didn't realise how completely my husband took control of everything, except the household affairs. Do you think I should tell the family doctor about my son?"

"I'm sure you should."

"Then I will," she decided.

Roger parked near Revel's office under the benevolent eye of a Divisional policeman, and went up to the top floor with the woman. Old Mr Revel himself was there, but the manager, Kent, was still off-duty. Roger checked one or two minor points, and left Mrs Bennison.

Simpson, brown trilby hat on the back of his head, and looking more rakish than raffish, was downstairs.

"What do you want me to do, Handsome?"

"Question all those witnesses again, and then try to have a word with everyone who saw or might have seen the lorry," Roger told him.

Prosy little Mrs Gossard had little to say in many words. She thought the drawings were "quite good". So did the porter whose oranges had been thrown all over the road. He repeated his story as if he had learned it off by heart.

The tall, burly-looking Calwin was striding along a side street with at least ten baskets of fruit on his head. He talked and behaved as if it were a skull cap.

"Thought it wouldn't be long before I seen you again," he declared. "Especially after the chap remembered that cove what had a thick ear. Got anyone yet?"

"I haven't found enough witnesses."

"Want more like me, that's what you want, 'Andsome." Calwin's impudence had a certain attractiveness. "Well, even I ain't made no progress, so don't fret yourself. I've been asking questions until they're sick of the sight of me—start pelting me with over-ripe melons if I go on much longer. To tell you the truth," he went on, actually lowering his head and so performing an incredible feat of balance with the baskets, "it was seeing Mrs Bennison what did it. 'Ow is she?"

"She'll make out."

"Musta give you a shock when she asked you why you let it happen," remarked Calwin sagely. "Any special line you'd like me to work on? No charge—all for love."

Roger said: "That cauliflower ear chap was probably a boxer. Talk it over with any fight fans in the market, will you?"

"Mixing business with pleasure that will be," said the porter. "Okay, guv'nor. Mind your 'ead." He gave a curious kind of body twist, lowered the baskets in his hands and placed them on the ground; they stood higher than he did himself. "Trust me!"

"What we want," Roger said to Simpson, "is plenty of these spread around." He took out prints of the composite pictures, without showing them directly to the porter. "How many can we put in the market?"

"A dozen of each, I'd say." Simpson decided.

"'Ere, let me look." Calwin peered down, breathing very heavily. After a long pause, he said: "Not *bad*. No, not bad, but not them, if you know what I mean."

The other witnesses all said virtually the same thing.

Roger went back to the office, reached there in the middle of the afternoon, and was not surprised to find a message: would he call Campbell, urgently. He needed no telling that Campbell was after results.

"The Old Man's getting really restive," the Deputy Commander complained. "Can you give me anything to pass on?"

"I'll send a set of those composite pictures," Roger promised. "That might help."

"Do that," said Campbell.

He hung up and Roger looked across at Cope's empty desk – Cope was somewhere in the building – sent for a messenger, and had him take the sketches up to the photographic department for more copies. When the telephone bell rang again, he looked at the instrument almost sourly, then picked it up.

"West speaking."

"Handsome, I think I've got something." It was Simpson again. "Calwin didn't lose much time. One of the Covent Garden fight fans thinks he's seen the man with the cauliflower ear before."

"Where is he?" Roger asked sharply.

"In my office, at this very moment."

"Send him over to the *Sporting World* offices in Fleet Street," Roger urged. "I'll meet him there. Have him ask for the assistant editor." He rang down on Simpson's "Right," and stood up, and took his hat off the hat stand, glad to be on the move again. He went across to Cope's desk, and was about to write a note when the door opened and Cope came in.

"What are you pinching?" he demanded.

"Be a help if you were around when you're wanted," Roger said. "I'll be at the *Sporting World* offices. Ring Medway and tell him I'm on my way, will you? I want a man to examine all the photographs of boxers who fought in the immediate past or are fighting these days. We've got a line."

Chapter Nine

Second Job

"All I've got to say is, I'm broke," said Mo Dorris. "I'm cleaned out."

"Then you're a fool," Marriott said.

"Take it easy, Win."

"You said you could stretch that money to last for three weeks. It's not a week yet."

"Well, I'm cleaned out."

"How'd you lose it?"

"Bloody dogs."

"I always told you—"

"What's the use of talking?" demanded Dorris. "I'm flat. You got ten quid you can lend me?"

Marriott said: "And what are you going to do for money after that?"

"That's not answering my question," Dorris said, resentfully. "Have you got ten nicker?"

"I could manage five."

"Five's no good."

"You haven't made yours last so long, have you?" jeered Marriott. Their friendship could be strained almost to breaking point over money, for Marriott was known to be very mean, whereas Dorris was an easy spender.

"You know what? We ought to pull another job, that's what."

Marriott rubbed his square chin.

"You're not going to let big-head Stevens stop you, are you?"

"No one's going to stop me. I'll do what I want to do."

"So what's the delay? It's been nearly a week, now, and we haven't had any trouble. Not a single question asked. There's nothing to worry about."

"We're in the clear, all right," Marriott said.

"So what's stopping us?"

In fact, the menace in Stevens's voice and eyes when he had last spoken to them, was stopping Marriott. He did not want to admit it. He wanted to pretend even to himself that whatever he did was entirely of his own volition. Yet he sensed that Dorris was in a bad temper, and would soon realise the truth. It was his boast that he wouldn't knuckle under to anyone.

"Okay," said Marriott, speaking slowly so as to cover the quick succession of his thoughts. "What's stopping us? But we've got to be careful."

"Of *him?*"

"Who cares about him? We've got to watch out, though, the cops aren't fools. We want to do a different kind of job."

Dorris leaned back in a chair in the room he shared with a younger brother, who was out, and asked brusquely:

"Okay, so long as it's a job. Got any ideas?"

"What ships are due in?" asked Marriott.

"Couple of Dutchmen and an Elder Dempster Line from Australia."

"That's the one we want to watch," said Marriott. Now that he had gone so far, much of his self confidence returned. "They have plenty of dough to come from those long trips. Where's she tying up?"

"Milner's."

"Sure?"

"I'm working her."

"Okay," said Marriott, his voice going very hard. "We'll pick off a couple of the A.B.'s off the E.D. What's she called?"

"The *Tropics*."

"We'll make it hot all right." Marriott giggled with laughter. "You find out what time they're paying off the crew, and knock off half an hour earlier than that, and be at the Cut as they pass through. Okay?"

"Now you're talking," Dorris said. "Some of these chaps draw a couple've hundred quid. Last us for another three or four weeks, that would."

Marriott did not think of the obvious retort then. Later, if all went well, and when Dorris had spent his share of the money, he would talk sarcastically about three or four weeks lasting only three or four *days,* but now he was planning and scheming – now he was the man in charge again. He forgot Stevens, for the time being; but once or twice during the day he thought uneasily about him, especially once when he caught sight of Alec Gool, nipping by on a motor-scooter. That was something new, Alec had invested some of the proceeds from the Covent Garden job.

Arthur Christie, able seaman on board the S.S. *Tropics,* was one of the best liked although one of the most frugal men on board the ship, which had a crew of fifty-one. It had been away from London for over five months, and had called at most Australian ports, at Samoa, Singapore, Hong Kong, before coming up through Suez, and the baking heat of the Red Sea. Although Christie had gone ashore at every port, he had spent very little money, and none at all on women. He was going to get married at the end of this trip.

In fact, he was going to get married on Saturday.

His shipmates knew that, although he had no idea that they were planning to club together and buy him a television set for a wedding present – to keep his new wife out of mischief when he was at sea, the gift note would say. He knew that the steamship company would give him a handsome cash present, for he had worked for them for seven years. By taking very little of his wages while at sea and in port, he had a tidy lot to come – well over two hundred pounds.

He had only ten minutes to walk from Milner Dock to Risher Street, where he lived and where Millie would be waiting for him.

True, he had to go through the Cut, and at night he would not have ventured there alone, but in broad daylight there would be nothing to worry about.

He collected his money, shook hands with those of the crew he knew well, and went off. No one actually stood on deck to watch him, and he felt a little disappointed. Usually any member of the crew who was going to get married before signing on again, got a big send-off. He was much more concerned about seeing Millie, however, and the indifference of everyone else did not make him downhearted for long. He had no idea that the indifference was deliberate, and that crowded in one of the galleys, some members of the crew were roaring their heads off about him. Their present attitude would make the television surprise packet even more complete.

The tired-looking sergeant-at-arms was at the foot of the gangway. Two cranes were working the holds, as well as the ship's derricks.

"You off, Art?"

"That's right, Sam."

"Do right by that girl of yours, now."

"Didn't anyone tell you?—I'm going to marry her."

They both laughed.

Christie walked very quickly over the steep rails on which the cranes ran, then between the warehouses, then towards the Gut, which was a narrow alley between warehouses; once upon a time it had been a narrow stream. It was a cool, rather blustery day near the end of August, but his thoughts of Millie were warming, and he did not give much thought to the hot weather he had left behind. He did wonder whether Millie might agree to go and settle in Australia or New Zealand, but there was plenty of time to decide that.

He entered the Cut.

It was gloomy along there, and the black cobbles were more uneven than he remembered. He couldn't hurry, and haste was all that mattered. Half way along, he thought he saw a movement ahead, and frowned – then a few yards further along, he did see one.

There was Millie!

She wore a dark raincoat pressed against her body by the wind which cut off the river, and a small hat framing her oval face. She was pretty enough, and to him she looked quite beautiful. Her eyes were huge. The moment she saw him, she began to run, high heels slipping on the cobbles so that once she almost fell. Christie broke into a run. They met in the middle of the Cut, flinging their arms round each other, kissing wildly, hugging, saying incoherent things. When at last they finished they were breathless and gasping. Millie was a little giggly.

They linked arms, but had to press very close together in order to walk along. Christie's left elbow scraped painfully along the brick wall of the warehouse, but he did not care, nothing mattered but the fact that Millie had come rushing here the moment she knew the *Tropics* was tied up. Christie was staring into her eyes, she was staring into his, and there was no one else in the world – when they reached the end of the Cut.

There was a scuffle of movement.

Christie jerked his head round. "What—" he began.

He saw two men, with scarves over their faces, and knew in a flash what they were after. He and Millie were still in the mouth of the Cut, and he had no freedom of action. Quick as a flash, he pushed her behind him. As he did so, a man raised his right hand; there was a bar of iron in it – angle iron. Millie screamed. Christie thrust out his right foot, and rammed it towards the attacker's stomach, but the man was prepared for that, changed the direction of his blow, and smashed the iron down on to Christie's knee. Agonising pain shot through the sailor's leg, and he pitched downwards.

"Let him alone!" Millie screamed. *"Let him alone!"*

She flung herself forward.

One of the men went down on his knees and started rooting in Christie's pockets. The other jumped at Millie. She did not back away, but struck out wildly. Her fingers caught the scarf which covered the lower part of his face. It twisted round, and dropped down. She saw his ugly battered face, saw his fist coming at her like a great bony ball. She tried to dodge, but the blow caught her high on the breast and sent her staggering backwards. As she gasped, she heard one of the men say: "I got it. Come on!"

She pitched backwards, hit her head on the cobbles, and lay dazed for several minutes until, half sobbing, she tried to scramble to her feet. By then people were hurrying towards the spot. She saw them a long way off, but all she really saw was her Arthur, lying huddled in front of her, his head turned to one side, his lips parted, his eyes closed – and a trickle of blood coming from the wound in his head, blood which already matted his hair.

Chapter Ten

Identification

Roger got out of his car opposite the *Sporting World's* offices, left the driver to park where he could and hurried inside. This was one of the older buildings of Fleet Street, and compared with the pallid-faced modern masses of concrete, glass and pseudo marble, looked an anachronism; there was nothing attractive about the Victorian frosted glass, the wooden hand-rails, the narrow dark passages and staircases. The lift was just big enough for three, at a squeeze. A man and a woman were already in it when Roger arrived, and looked apprehensively as he stepped in, massive and heavy compared with them. The lift crawled.

"I think perhaps the load's a bit heavy," the woman said, timidly.

"They really ought to get a new one."

"I *did* hear that they were going to pull this down next year and put a twenty storey building in its place. I don't know what London's coming to. These big square box-like buildings are ruining the city."

To their obvious relief, Roger got out at the second floor. A nice-looking young girl wearing a white blouse comfortably filled and with her hair unexpectedly prim and Edwardian style, smiled at him with commercial television brightness.

"Superintendent West?"

"Yes."

"Mr Medway is expecting you. Come this way, please."

As they walked along, shoulders touching, she glanced up at him once or twice. Then she opened a door marked *Assistant Editor.*

Medway, short, tubby, always dressed in loud clothes, a bit horsey and a bit sporty as a cunning *aide* to his profession, had the roundest, baldest, pinkest head of any Roger knew. It bobbed out from behind the ungainly figure of the Covent Garden porter, Galwin. With Calwin was another man, dressed in a pair of thick serge trousers and wearing a thick navy type jersey of faded blue. This stranger had a craggy face and very shaggy eyebrows, with eyes which sparkled deep in little pits of sockets.

"Hallo, Handsome." Medway held out his hand.

"Didn't expect me, did you?" Calwin grinned. He looked uglier every time Roger saw him. "Meet my pal, Joey Lark."

"*Lark,*" echoed Medway, closing his eyes.

"Twenty years ago he was the best light-weight in the business, wasn't he, Mr Medway?"

Medway said hurriedly: "One of the very best." His expression seemed to ask: "Why did you wish this lot on to me, Handsome?"

Roger managed to say hello, grin at Calwin, and hold out his hand to Joey Lark at one and the same time. Lark's craggy face had a familiar look. There was something forthright and honest about his gaze, too, something foursquare about his stocky figure. His hair, iron grey, was curly and rather long.

"Please to meet you, Superintendent," Lark said. His hand grip was almost fervent.

"So you think you can help us," Roger remarked.

"Wouldn't be here if we didn't," said Calwin. "I took those pretty pictures of yourn round to the boxing boys, like you told me, and Joey picked out the boxer. Said he was sure he's seen 'im before, but couldn't remember his name."

"What we would like to do, Med," Roger said to the assistant editor, "is go through your Boxers' Gallery, so that Mr Lark can pick out the man he thinks the drawing represents. It might take a long time, but would be well worth doing."

"The gallery's yours," said Medway.

"Don't forget it's overtime rates," put in Calwin.

"Dry up, Cal," Lark said, in his rather quiet voice. "If I can help the police I don't want paying for it."

"More fool you," retorted Calwin. "Overtime *and* expenses I want!" He gave a vast grin. "Lead on, McDuff."

Medway rolled his eyes.

In a long, narrow room, like a section of *Records* at the Yard, were shelves upon shelves of files, each filled with photographs. It was bewildering to think that so many boxing hopes actually got as far as getting their photographs taken for newspaper use. At one end of the room was a long desk, which sloped downwards, with several stools at it. Roger waited until Calwin was settled at one, Lark at another, and one of the *Sporting World's* junior librarians ready to feed them with photographs.

"It might take half the night as well as the rest of the day," Medway said. "If we get anything we'll call you, Handsome."

"Thanks," said Roger, and added in an undertone: "See that they get anything they want, won't you?"

"It'll be on the house," Medway assured him. "I can see the headlines. Killer traced through *Sporting World*. I can show you one photo that may surprise you, too." He went to a shelf and took down a file while Lark and Calwin began turning photographs over, and scrutinising the faces. Medway flipped several to one side, and held one out to Roger. It was of a tall, powerful-looking man in an old fashioned boxing stance. He was wearing trunks and slippers and gloves, just as if he was about to enter the ring. There was something vaguely familiar about him.

He turned it over.

Charley Blake, Navy Middleweight Champion, at the time he turned professional.

There were a lot of other details about Blake – height, weight, amateur fights, but the significant thing was his name. This was the man whom Roger had seen only once, on a mortuary slab; the man knifed in that sudden, merciless attack outside the bank in Covent Garden.

"Wonder if it means anything," Medway said. "You're looking for a pug, and Blake was one in his young days."

"Worth thinking about," Roger agreed. He remembered that Blake had been ex-Navy and ex-Merchant Navy, turned it over in his mind as he went out with Medway at his side. As they approached the assistant editor's door, the nice-looking girl came out.

"Your office would like to speak to you, Mr West."

"Oh. Thanks."

It was Cope.

"Been a job over at the docks I thought you ought to know about," said Cope, without preamble. "Sailor just come off a ship smacked over the head, and robbed of all the cash he'd brought home with him – two hundred quid. His fiansey had gone to meet him, and she was knocked about too – but she saw one of the assailants."

Cope paused, significantly.

"Well?"

"The way she described him he could fit in with one of the four we're looking for on the Covent Garden job," said Cope. "The bruiser with the cauliflower ear."

"I'll go and see her at once," Roger said quickly. "How's the injured man?"

"Dunno," said Cope.

"Where is he?"

"Mile End Hospital."

"Ask someone from the Division to meet me there," said Roger. "Send the girl there too, if she can get about."

"Right-i-ho." Cope hung up, while Medway looked curiously at Roger, who felt a growing excitement and tension, although outwardly that showed only in a tightening of his lips and a narrowing of his eyes; at moments like these he looked as if he were staring into distant places. This looked like the luck he had been praying for; two breaks at the same time.

"Anything important?" asked Medway.

"Could be," said Roger. "Thanks a lot for your help, Med. I'll keep you out of prison one day."

Medway was laughing when they shook hands.

Twenty minutes later Roger stepped into the main entrance of the Mile End Hospital, that oasis of healing and repair work in the heart of the East End. A rather short, very thickset man, Golloway of the East End Division, was talking to three younger men – obviously newspaper men. He saw Roger and seemed to shrug the others aside, came forward walking with a kind of rhinoceros gait, and held out a thick, brick-red hand.

"How's your invalid?" Roger inquired.

"He'll do," said Golloway. "It could have been a lot worse – he'll be up and about inside a week. But I've got what you asked for." He lowered his voice. "Spare a minute for the Press, first?"

"Yes." Roger turned and put on his newspaper smile, answered a few not very intelligent questions, then went out of the hall with Golloway, into a small room where a middle-aged woman in a blue gown and white head-dress was waiting.

"Sister Lee," Golloway introduced, "Superintendent West."

"Good afternoon, Mr West." Her hand was as cool as her voice and her appearance, and her manner was just on the thawing side of reserved. "Here are the two X-ray plates, for you to examine."

The photographs were on a stand with a lamp behind it, and she switched on. The two fractures – Bennison's and the one on the sailor whose name he did not yet know – showed up like the ghosts of skeletons. Roger knew enough about skull fractures to see the similarity, although the sailor had been lucky – the blow had been less savage, although vicious enough. As he compared them, the door opened and Simister came in. Roger saw the Sister's manner change and become subtly less assertive. Simister seemed very young in a close cut suit, and his hair made him look rather like the popular image of a musician.

He gave Sister Lee a quick, pleasant smile.

"Nice to see you again, Sister. Ah, there are the plates." He glanced at Roger and Golloway. "Good afternoon." He studied the plates intently, then took out a magnifying glass and held it in front of his right eye. When he drew back, he said without a moment's hesitation: "The wounds were caused with the same kind of weapon, probably a ridged piece of iron. Angle iron, possibly. I can't pretend to guess whether it was the same piece or whether it was struck by the same hand, of course."

"You've told us all we could hope for," Roger said. "Thanks. Golly, we want those two men more than we've wanted anyone for a long time. How much help do you need?"

"Can you find me a dozen chaps?"

"I'll get 'em over to you," Roger said, sure that Campbell would do anything to speed up results. "Who's over at the place where it happened?"

"Little—best man we've got for that area."

"Let's go and see him," said Roger, and then snapped his fingers at his own forgetfulness. "How about the girl? Is she badly hurt?"

"She was bruised on the chest, and on the back of the head where she struck the ground, but not seriously," Sister Lee told him. "She is in a waiting room near her fiancé."

"Has she seen one of those composite pictures?" Roger asked.

"Not yet," Golloway replied.

"Better show her one, now. Will you tell us where to go, Sister?"

"I will come with you," Sister Lee offered. "Mr Simister, while you are here I wonder if you would have a word with Dr Abrahams and Dr Moss. They are rather worried by the two victims of that bus and lorry accident this morning. There is some doubt as to whether the lorry driver died as a result of the accident or before it. If it was a heart spasm—"

"I'll see Dr Abrahams."

"Thank you."

Simister nodded to Roger and Golloway, who looked down his nose but said nothing. As they went up two flights of stairs, seeing a big lift carrying two stretchers and four nurses, Roger felt eagerness which eased tension in one way, and increased it in another. The feeling that they were on to one of the men was increasing all the time; and things were beginning to drop into place.

"If we don't get this chap soon, no telling what damage he might do," said Golloway. "Anyone who'll do this kind of job for a couple of hundred quid—" he glanced at Sister Lee, who was staring straight ahead. She had a fine, aquiline profile, and her cheeks were almost devoid of colour. "It's one thing to jump a man and rob him, but to go around with angle iron—"

"I know what you mean," Roger said. "Think things are worse or better than they used to be, Sister?"

She smiled with unexpected charm.

"In some ways worse, but in others a great deal better," she said. "I think we have more injuries to deal with because of crimes of violence, but I also think that the general attitude of people towards crime is different—more and more people are shocked by what is happening."

It was a shrewd summing up of the modern trend, Roger thought; the long hard battle against crime *was* gradually being won.

That was little consolation to the latest victims.

"Yes, that's like him," the girl said to Roger. She stared hard-eyed at the photograph of the composite picture. "It's *very* like him, especially that big swollen ear. And I'm sure there was a hole in it. Every time I close my eyes like Mr Golloway tells me, and try to picture the man's face, I see that little hole. I'm *sure* I'm right." She turned as eagerly to Sister Lee. "Sister, my fiancé will be all right, won't he?"

"He will be perfectly all right."

"Do you think he might be able to come out for Saturday?"

"Why? Is there anything special planned for Saturday?"

"Well, yes, there is, rather. You see, we were going to get married ..."

"Now we're moving," Roger said with brittle satisfaction. The call for Moses Dorris had already gone out, every policeman in this part of London was already on the look out for him. Four men had gone to the house where he lived with his old parents and a brother, in the hope that he would simply walk into their arms. All his known haunts, clubs, cafes, friends, were being checked. In its quiet way, this was one of the most thorough searches made in London for a long time. Roger had a sense that everyone in the Division was on his toes, and desperate for results; everyone on the Force seemed to sense that this was an unusual challenge.

"Shouldn't be long before we get him," Golloway said. He was a little pleased with himself, understandably. "Glad I recognised him from that girl's description."

"Damned good piece of work," Roger approved warmly. He was mildly amused by Golloway's obvious self-satisfaction.

They were in Golloway's office, at the East End Divisional Headquarters near Mile End Road. A tray of tea, with buns, cakes and sandwiches, was in front of them. He put a cup to his lips – and one of the telephones rang.

"Cope," said Golloway, and handed the receiver over.

"Yes, Jack?" Roger inquired.

"Here's a surprise for you," Cope said, sardonically. "Medway rang up, nearly as excited as Calwin. They've identified the man they were looking for. Name of Dorris."

"Did you tell them they were late?"

"Want me to?"

"No," said Roger. "Let 'em bask in their glory. And make sure a chit for a fiver goes to each."

"Needn't worry about depleting the public funds for them," said Cope. "Medway's paying 'em fifty quid each for an interview over this job."

"Then try depleting the public funds by a fiver to …" Roger gave the name of the injured sailor, laughed when Cope said that the cashier would never stand it, and went on: "If he won't, we'll club together, Jack—just you and me. This pair deserves a wedding present. Anything else in?"

Cope said: "Well, in a way."

There was something about the way he said that which warned Roger that the news wasn't good. In a brighter mood because of the sudden change of fortune, he did not want gloomy tidings, but whatever it was he had to take it. The quicker the better.

"What way?" he asked.

"I had a talk with Semple-Smith—he wanted to talk to you," reported Cope. "They can't save Bennison's right leg. He'll lose it above the knee. And they think he'll have permanent shoulder trouble, too—the right shoulder. Won't be able to move his arm much. He's in a mess, that poor devil is."

"And don't I know it?" Roger rang off slowly, stared out of the window, then went on to Golloway: "Bennison's going to lose a leg. Well! I mustn't spend any more time here. The moment you get your hands on Moses Dorris, give me a buzz, won't you? I'd like to be here when you start questioning him. You don't need telling that we want the names of the others. You can make him think he'll get a better deal if he names them quickly."

"Now, Handsome," said Golloway, grinning. "Is that ethical?"

"Anything that will help us get these swine is ethical for my money," Roger said.

It was an easy, even trite remark, but he found himself thinking about it as he was driven back to Scotland Yard. He would have preferred to stay in the East End, but it might be hours before Dorris was found, and if the man had the slightest warning, he might run to earth; if he did, it might take days to find him.

But he no longer felt that the case was turning sour.

Mrs Bennison would …

As he passed Aldgate East Station, he saw two Divisional and one Yard man mixing with the crowds which were already swelling to rush-hour magnitude, and he knew that they were looking for Moses, known as Mo Dorris. Would the luck hold? Would they get him quickly?

He saw another man, tall, rather distinguished in his way; head and shoulders physically and metaphorically above most of the people near him, he looked intelligent too. By this man's side was a youth, who might well be his son – slighter in build, very neatly dressed, with well groomed hair and a hint of superciliousness in his expression which somehow spoiled the impression he gave. The couple registered on Roger's mind although he saw them only for a few seconds, while the car was held by the traffic.

Soon, he forgot them.

Chapter Eleven

Kill

"Don't look now," Alec Gool said, "but there's that copper, West. In the black Rover."

He glanced up at Stevens's face, and saw the taller man's eyes swivel round, but he did not turn his head until they were a few yards on. Then he bought a newspaper, and took the opportunity to stare along the rows of traffic. Buses were rumbling, there was a crawling line of diesel lorries and trucks stretching for a hundred yards, cyclists and motor-scooterists were threading their way through the crowd, workers were already thronging into and out of the station.

"See him?" asked Alec.

"Saw the back of his head. Are you sure?"

"I'm sure all right," said Gool. "Wonder what he's doing out here."

"It needn't worry us," Stevens said. They crossed the narrow end of Middlesex Street, where there was not a single stall to remind anyone that it became Petticoat Lane on Sunday. As they did so, a small boy came up to them, curly-haired, grubby-looking, with wide, innocent eyes.

Alec caught Steve's arm, with unexpected tightness.

"That's Marriott's kid," he said hurriedly.

"My Dad says he wants to see you two," the boy said, in a piping voice. "He says, will you go to the Chink's place."

"Okay, son," said Steve. He dipped his hand into his pocket, produced a shilling, and tossed it into the air; Marriott's son snatched it expertly, and without saying a word, turned and lost himself in the crowd.

"Now what's on?" Alec asked.

"We'll find out," said Steve. "You ask around, I'll go and see Marriott."

Alec said: "I don't like it."

"What don't you like?"

"The Chink's place," he said. "You know it's—"

"I know it's a Chinese restaurant where they serve lousy American-Chinese food."

"You don't know about the cellar," Alec said. "It's a hide-out. I don't like it, I tell you. If you ask me, I ought to go to the Chink's place, you ought to keep away."

"I'm going," Steve insisted.

The Chink's place was in the middle of a small row of shops in a side street leading off the Mile End Road. It had yellow lace curtains in the window, Chinese lettering and signs in gold paint, fly-spotted menus stuck by drying Scotch tape in the windows. Steve had to duck in order to get in. There were twenty or so tables, several of them occupied, mostly by Chinese and Indian sailors, who could get a semblance of the food they preferred in this place. Three diminutive Chinese men were waiting for more custom. The oldest of them came forward, a little podge in a pale grey suit and with a very shiny face. His eye-lids were puffy, and almost hid his eyes.

"You come in plivate dining room," he said. "I got velly spleshul eats for you." He gave a slight bow, and pushed a curtain aside. Behind was a small room, with three tables laid, but no one was in it. Steve had not been in here before, and, but for Alec's warning, he would have been taken completely by surprise. The Chinese took him out by another door, and pushed open a third. A dim light shone on steep cellar steps.

Steve thought: "That kid's got the right kind of nose."

He went downstairs, bending low, because the ceiling was almost head height. The lights were subdued, but the atmosphere was quite fresh. Ching stayed behind him, but as he reached the foot of the stone steps, Marriott bobbed out of a doorway on the right.

Marriott looked small and scared.

"Where the hell have you been?" he muttered. "I thought you were never coming."

"Don't you talk to me—" Steve began, and then checked himself. He could deal with this man when he knew what it was all about, there was no point in starting a shouting match at this stage. The impulse died. "What's the matter?" he demanded. "Trouble?"

Marriott said: "The cops are looking for Mo and me."

Steve didn't speak.

"You gone deaf?"

He was scared, Steve knew, so scared that he was almost beside himself. This was so bad that it could hardly be worse. Steve had to bite on his words as he pushed forward into the main cellar. Mo Dorris was standing by a dim electric light, which had no shade. Above him was a thick glass hatch, and footsteps sounded over his head. This cellar was jutting out into the street.

"I can hear," Steve said. "So they're on to you."

"We've got to get away," Dorris said hoarsely. "You've got to find us somewhere to hide until we can get a boat. You flicking swine."

Steve stared at him.

"If you hadn't killed that guard—" Dorris began, and then swallowed his words.

"So I killed the guard," Steve said, thinly. "And you nearly killed the other man, don't forget that. You're in it as deep as I am." The words were empty and wasted; Dorris knew just how deep he was in this – so far as the police were concerned. Perhaps he also suspected what was going through his, Steve's mind; possibly he had realised what Steve would think, that might explain the coldness of his fear. "How bad is it?" Steve made himself sound calm and co-operative.

"Couldn't be worse," Marriott answered. "The cops are waiting at Mo's place—*and* at mine. I sent my kids to look out for you and Alec. If you hadn't been away—"

"We went to the Oval," Steve said. "When I have to ask your permission to go and watch a cricket match, that will be the day. Where else are the police?"

"They're at …" – Marriott answered, and named all the places which they frequented; the cafe with the three bouncy waitresses, the Hornpipe, the club, half a dozen other haunts. As he talked, the picture became more vivid. The police were spreading the net so wide that Dorris couldn't escape it, and there was no doubt that it was for the Covent Garden job. Dorris was known to be an associate of Marriott, so Marriott's friends, his wife, his children, were being questioned, too. A friend – one of the waitresses at the cafe – had tipped them off.

"So we came here," Marriott said. "Steve, we've got to get a ship."

"The two of you?"

"It stands to reason !"

"We've got to get out of England until it's all blown over," Marriott said. He licked his lips. "They've got photographs, God knows how." He gulped. "Listen, Steve, we need some dough. If we can get some dough we'll be okay."

"The two hundred won't be enough," Dorris said, and Marriott looked at him sharply.

Steve stood very still, top of his head almost touching the ceiling, eyes narrowed as his gaze switched from one man to the other. Footsteps were going more quickly: tap-tap-tap-tap-thump-thump-thump. A car roared.

"What two hundred?" Steve asked, flatly.

"We – we still got a couple of hundred between us," Marriott said, almost desperately. "All we need is—"

"*What* two hundred? You were almost spent out yesterday. Mo tried to borrow five nicker from Alec. What—"

"We—we—we did a job. It was easy, we didn't have any trouble, if it hadn't been for the girl …"

As Dorris was gasping out the explanation, his fear of Steve at least as great as his fear of the police at that moment, Steve Stevens came to the positive knowledge of what he must do. It wasn't impulse; it was cold, calculated decision.

He had to make sure that these two men could not talk. They had to be killed.

"You know what they did?" Alec asked. They were together in the saloon bar of a pub in the Whitechapel Road, not far from the Chink's place. "They did a sailor off the *Tropics*. Got away with two hundred quid. The sailor's girl went to meet him, and she clawed the scarf off Dorris's face. A *girl* did that. So she identified him. Who wouldn't? He's dangerous, Steve. They're both dangerous. If the cops get them they'll bring us in, and the cops will catch up with them sooner or later. They're too well known. As it is, we've been seen with them too often already."

Steve said: "I know."

"They've got to go, Steve."

"They're on their way," Steve said. He tossed down a whisky. "How safe is the Chink?"

"He's okay for tonight," Alec said. "You know where that cellar leads to, don't you?"

"Tell me."

"One of the old sewers which used to empty themselves in the Thames."

"Well?"

"At low tide, that'll be around eleven o'clock tonight, you can walk along these sewers, and be picked up by a boat," said Alec. "It's easy. The Chink makes his money that way—he gets a hundred every time he helps someone out. They've got to lay on the ship." Alec drank light ale, as if he were enjoying the bouquet. "There's a Liberian freighter going out tonight—the *Glambia*. Its first port of call is Freetown, on the West African coast."

Steve said: "Do you want to pay their passage money?"

"You get me wrong," said Alec. "Our boys know the ship's due out, they know the captain will take on deckhands without asking too many questions. If we tell them they're going on the *Glambia,* they'll buy it. We can make sure they don't reach the ship."

Steve was smiling a tense, thin-lipped smile, and he caught sight of his reflection in a decorated mirror, very like the one in which he often saw Joyce. He thought of Joyce; he wanted to see Joyce now.

"Okay?" asked Alec.

"So far. What are the weak points?"

"We've got to fool Marriott into thinking he can see his wife before he goes on board, otherwise he'll try to go and see her at home, and the cops will pick him up. Dorris won't care if he never sees his Ma and Pa again. They won't care if they don't see him, either. Okay?"

"Could be," said Steve.

"What's on your mind?"

"If they are picked up dead, the police will know someone killed them."

"Not the way I've got it worked out," said Alec. His lips twisted first into a smirk of satisfaction then in a smile of delight. He had shaved since getting back from the Oval, and his hair was almost femininely groomed, while the hand which closed about the glass was white and delicate-looking. "We fix it with the captain of the *Glambia*. He gets fifty quid for the job of taking them away if they reach the ship. They start out in a dinghy, but they don't get far. That dinghy's got a hole in it, plugged with cork which will burst soon after they start off. We'll fix a hole in it. I happen to know a lot about that pair," Alec went on. He smiled like an angel into Steve's face. "I happen to know they can't swim, for instance. It's a long way from the river bank to the *Glambia*—she's tied up at Nix's, the Thames is very wide there. It's a deserted part of the river where this sewer goes out, too. They won't ever make it."

"If a ship's passing, or a police launch—"

"Steve," said Alec, with the manner of a man twice the other's age, "we can't expect a hundred per cent certainty. This one's ninety-nine per cent."

Steve stared at the mirror. After a long while, he asked:

"What's heavy that the master of the *Glambia* would like to have? Something our boys could carry in their shoes, or in their clothes?"

"No good," said Alec. "The cops would find—"

"Would that matter? The cops know they're planning to go out of the country, they won't be surprised at what they have in their pockets—or what they're trying to smuggle out of the country. Lead would do the trick, but it's not valuable enough."

"I know where I can lay my hands on some 'gold'—or something that looks like gold," Alec broke in softly. "Lead with gold leaf round it, made like a body bet. It clips round the small of the back." He demonstrated. "It was brought in by some lascars who'd paid real money for it in Beira—thought it was genuine. Our boys will fall for it, but can we get the dough?"

"I can get enough for this job," Steve said. "I don't spend my last penny."

At eleven o'clock that night the telephone bell rang in the Wests' home. Martin, the elder boy, was reading in the kitchen. He looked up, obviously hoping that one of the others would answer the telephone. His father was in the front room, Richard and his mother were upstairs, Richard trying on a shirt which wanted the sleeves shortening. He could hear his mother calling out:

"Don't, Richard! Stand still."

Richard was in one of his giggly moods, then.

The telephone bell kept ringing. At last, Martin, called Scoop, a broad-shouldered, physically strong and very fit lad, put his book down reluctantly, and got up. As he did so, he heard his father answer.

"Roger West speaking."

Martin went to the door, the tone of voice intriguing him. He saw his father standing in the hallway, where a telephone was easily accessible to all parts of the ground floor. He saw from his father's expression that this was something which really mattered to him. They had seen very little of each other lately, and although Martin knew about the Bennison job, he had no idea how deeply it mattered.

"Oh, well," his father said. "Tomorrow's another day. No sign at all, you say." He held on for a moment, then straightened up, and said: "Goodnight. Thanks." He put down the receiver and stared straight ahead for a few seconds, as if he did not notice his son.

Then Scoop heard his mother shout from the top of the stairs: "Any luck, dear?"

"They haven't got either of them yet," Roger replied. "I'm beginning to think they might have been tipped off."

"Is it anything important?" Martin inquired.

"Pretty important," his father said. "When you hear the telephone ring, don't wait for an hour before answering it."

"Sorry, Dad," Martin said guiltily.

"I can tell you're worried, Dad," Richard put in. He had come down to distract attention from his brother. "Is it this Bennison job?"

"Yes, that's it," Roger said.

Suddenly he began to talk, as he would sometimes to the family, about Bennison, young Paul Bennison, that family, the day's hope that they were on the right track, and now the failure to pick up the boxer, Dorris, or his close friend, Marriott. Richard, taller than Scoop, with thick dark hair, and intent manner, listened enthralled.

Talking was doing Roger good, Janet persuaded herself.

As Roger talked, the *Glambia* sailed slowly downstream, with the pilot on board, all her lights on, new paint glistening beneath these lights.

And as he talked, Mo Dorris and Win Marriott climbed into the little boat which was to take them across to the *Glambia*. There would be no difficulty about getting aboard, they believed – a rope ladder would be trailing from the stern, and the vessel did not stand high out of the water now she was fully loaded.

Marriott was sulking because his wife hadn't come, as Steve had promised. He kept looking up at the river bank.

Two bands of "gold" clipped round his middle, made him feel heavy and cumbersome, but also made him feel as if he was worth a fortunc, even shared with the *Glambia's* skipper. That Steve was a close one, to have the money available. Marriott saw the red glow of a cigarette not far away, and went rigid with fear.

"See that?" he whispered.

"Shurrup," muttered Dorris. "I've got to start rowing." He took the sculls as he settled in the thwarts. "Lot of water in her." Water was in fact swirling about their feet. He judged the distance to the *Glambia*. "Stop moving around," he said testily. "We've got to make it."

Marriott sat down.

A few minutes later, he said: "The water's up to my ankles. What did they get us this colander for?"

"It's okay. It—"

A curious plopping sound cut across the words. They did not know that it was the cork, forced out by the pressure of the water round the uneven edge, but almost at once the water rose to their calves, and suddenly Marriott gasped:

"We're sinking."

"Don't be a bloody fool! We won't sink—"

"It's going down under us," Marriott gasped. "I can't swim. God! This gold will sink us. God!"

He began to tear at his clothes, but swayed to one side. The boat rolled over, shipping so much water that it capsized with frightening suddenness. The cold, oily, muddy water of the Thames closed over Marriott as his mouth was open to cry out in panic. He retched and began to struggle, but the heavy cloth was too wet, he couldn't pull the sleeves off. Dorris heard a groaning kind of shout, and knew that it was Marriott. He caught sight of Win's arms waving, already thirty or forty feet away from him. He didn't shout back, didn't open his mouth, he was so afraid of swallowing water. Fear was tearing at him wildly, and something near panic was about him – but his training for the ring helped to keep him steady, helped him to fight for his life.

These bloody gold belts …

A small freighter, coming up stream, caused a wake which suddenly lifted Dorris up several feet, then plunged him under. His mouth opened. He knew the terror of approaching death, began to strike out, to kick out, even tried to *scream*.

Chapter Twelve

Boy Lost

Roger stepped into his office, at half past eight next morning, and saw Cope already at his desk, collar loose, tie hanging down. It was hot and sultry. Cope looked up, and simply shook his head. Roger had anticipated that; if either of the wanted men had been discovered he would have heard the moment he stepped into the building. Yet he was acutely disappointed. The post, unopened, lay on his desk. A telephone bell rang, and before he took off his hat he picked up the receiver; hope rose again.

"Handsome." It was Campbell, probably speaking from home. "Have we got Dorris or Marriott?"

"Not yet," Roger said. He sat on a corner of the desk. "And if the Old Man wants quicker results, he'll have to find someone else to get them for him. I'm at full stretch."

"Now take it easy," protested Campbell. "I have to call him at his home. All the stops are out, aren't they?"

"Every stop I know about," Roger said. He was twisting round awkwardly. "There's a file on my desk which says: *Dorris and Marriott—known associates.* It's as thick as your fist."

"All right," said Campbell. "I'll be in by ten o'clock."

Roger rang off, slapped his hat on a peg, then squatted at the corner of the table again and opened the file, the words on which had been upside down to him.

"Anything in this, Jack?"

"Dunno, yet. Golloway sent it up, by a messenger. He's probably demonstrating that he's right on the ball."

"Glad someone is," Roger said. He studied the report closely, and had to admit that Golloway was not only on the ball but was on top of his job. He had prepared a short dossier on Dorris, Marriott, and their families, friends and acquaintances. Each was on a separate piece of paper, which accounted for the thickness of the file. Special reference was made to their families – Marriott's wife and three children, the youngest a boy of eight – Dorris's old mother and father and a married sister, as well as a brother a few years younger than he. The dossiers included the places where all of these went to work (or to school if they were young), where they were likely to be found for drinks, what clubs they belonged to. At the top of each dossier was a note of the name and address, there was a brief description of the physical appearance and in many cases photographs were pinned to the top left hand corner.

"Any good?" Cope inquired.

"He must have had a couple of typists up all night for this job," said Roger. "Go through it, will you?" He pulled a telephone to him, asked for Golloway, and was told that he was not yet in. "As soon as he arrives ask him if he can fill up gaps in the photographs of the people in his files as soon as possible."

"Very good, sir."

Roger rang off, and opened other files, some of them dealing with different cases. Nothing was helpful. He reported again to Campbell, who was increasingly gloomy about the failure to find the two wanted men. A morning which had started with disappointment grew into a day of greater disappointment, for after all the photographs had come in from Golloway, none of the known friends and acquaintances of Dorris or Marriott resembled either of the other men seen at the Covent Garden crime.

"Those two descriptions were pretty vague," Cope pointed out, and did not greatly ease the situation.

Twice during the day false hopes were raised. By six o'clock, every known or suspected hiding place had been searched, but there was no sign of the missing men. Golloway sent in a note: "*A Liberian freighter, the* Glambia, *sailed on the night tide last night. Our men could have been aboard."* Had there been the slightest evidence Roger would have had the ship radio'd, but it was sheer guesswork.

Just before six, when he was ready to leave, his telephone bell rang.

"Mrs Bennison would like to speak to you, sir," the operator said.

"Put her through," said Roger, automatically.

He held on for a few moments, wondering what she would want; he had always told her that if she needed any help that he could give, she had only to ask him for it. This might mean anything – the one thing he took for granted was that it would not be pointless. He had not inquired about Bennison for the last day or two. Since the news of the amputation of his right leg, nothing new had been reported. Semple-Smith had not been in touch with Simister lately, and as he held on Roger had a half guilty feeling, that he should have inquired further about the effect on the brain.

At heart, of course, he did not want to admit the possibility of idiocy.

"Mr West?" The moment he heard the woman's voice, he was sure that there was an emergency.

"Hallo, Mrs Bennison."

"Mr West, Paul has run away!"

Roger thought: "Run away", blankly. Paul Junior, of course, but – run *away*? He could picture those dark, intent eyes, eyes which did not show any expression and which had turned slaty grey in the boy's determination to remain aloof.

"When did you last see him?" Roger inquired, still mechanically. He was trying to see the significance of this, beyond the fact that it might drive Isobel Bennison to desperation.

"This morning," she answered. "He went out for the day—he told me he was going to the Oval, to see a cricket game." "Game" was a woman's word for "match", the word Janet often used in spite of the scoffing of her three "men". He left early, and I took it for granted that he meant what he said. But he didn't go to the Oval."

"Are you sure?"

"Yes, I'm absolutely sure. He was to have met some friends when he got there. He told them that he would be late and couldn't travel with them. He was to have been at the gasometer scoreboard. Does that mean anything to you?"

"It means a great deal," Roger assured her. "How many other boys were there?"

"Four. They were all neighbours' children. Paul has been so strange lately that I asked Mrs Abbott—you met her, didn't you?" Mrs Bennison gave Roger no time to answer, but went on breathlessly: "I asked her if she would get her boys and some others in the street to organise a party somewhere. Paul's always been fond of cricket. His father, too. And he seemed to jump at the chance. I don't know what's happened to him, he's been so strange—"

"Have you told anyone else about this?" Roger interrupted.

"No, no one."

"I shall telephone the local police at once, and I'll be over myself in half an hour or so," Roger said. "Don't talk to anyone else yet, will you?"

"I'll do whatever you say," Isobel Bennison promised.

Cope, still at his desk, had obviously gathered the drift of this. Roger told him to contact the Wimbledon Division, so that the search for the lad could be started at once.

"And have a word with the Kennington Division and check the Oval," Roger said. "We want that boy's movements traced from the time he left home at half past eleven this morning. Have we got his description?"

"A vague one," Cope said.

"Take this down. Aged twelve, could pass for fourteen or fifteen. Five feet six or seven. Slender build. Very dark hair, left side parting, hair inclined to curl at the temples but usually kept fairly flat. Grey to dark grey eyes. Rather good-looking, you might say Gregory Peckish. I don't know what clothes he was wearing—ring Mrs Bennison herself about that. Don't let the Press get hold of the story." Roger was already at the door, but suddenly checked himself. "One other thing—small scar on the lobe of the left ear. Oh, and he had long—exceptionally long—thumbs. Got it?"

"Yep."

"Call my home for me and tell Janet I'll be late-ish, will you?"

"Okay," said Cope.

Roger drove himself again, conscious of the busy, impatient rush hour traffic, which was only just beginning to tail off. From the moment he had seen Bennison's son, he had been troubled by him. His reactions hadn't been normal even allowing for shock from the news of the injuries to his father. Shocks like this usually brought out whatever was latent in a human being, they put nothing new in. What would the boy do? Was he bitterly disappointed because the police had not yet made an arrest? Could he possibly have conceived some foolish idea of looking for the men himself? It wasn't rational, Roger knew; but little about this case was rational.

He found the traffic thinning as he drove through Fulham and Putney, and had a fairly quick run up the hill. Soon, just beyond the common, he was in Acacia Avenue. No little crowd stood about near the Bennisons' gate; it looked as if the public interest in them was satiated.

The garage doors were closed, the garden gate and windows were closed, too. The house had a deserted appearance.

Roger wondered suddenly whether the boy had been found, and his mother was on her way to him, but as he went up the path to the front door, it opened. Isobel Bennison stood there for a moment, her hands half raised in front of her. She was looking very, very tired.

"There isn't—isn't any news of him?" she asked, half hopefully, half despairing.

"There soon will be," Roger said. The inadequacy of the remark irritated him, but he had to say something. The woman stood there and he saw that she was frightened as well as tired. She did not move. He took her right arm, and turned her round slowly and gently. She began to walk mechanically, passing the front room along to the kitchen quarters. The silence of emptiness lay upon the house.

"Where are the others?" Roger asked, searching for their names. "Michael and—Michael and *Rose.*"

101

JOHN CREASEY

"They're staying with their grandmother," answered Isobel. "They usually go to her for a week in the summer, and this was the time we'd arranged. Paul wouldn't go. He said—he said he had to stay at home and look after me. I couldn't *make* him go, could I?"

"Of course not."

She began to walk about the kitchen, picking things up, putting them down. She was nearer distraught than Roger had realised, and he wondered if anything else was worrying her. He wished she would do something: make some tea or coffee, get a drink, anything.

She talked all the time.

"I'm glad you agree—some of the neighbours think I ought to have made him go. I can't even be sure why I didn't. Am I being selfish? I hate the thought of being here alone, and—well, Paul is more like my husband. Rose tries so hard, bless her, but she isn't much help. She's younger than her years, and keeps trying to comfort me by using phrases out of books." Isobel stopped in front of Roger, looking straight into his eyes. "It's been terrible on my own, especially since—"

She broke off, hands working, lips working. She turned her back to him, and put her hands to her eyes. He moved forward and rested a hand on her shoulder, a token of comfort. He had never felt more troubled about anyone, man or woman, outside his own family. He felt the trembling of her body as she fought back tears, and sensed that she was very close to complete collapse.

"I don't know what's coming over me," she said, in a shaking voice. "Worrying about myself when Paul's missing. Oh, *God.*" She made those two short words sound like a prayer deep from the heart. Roger's hand pressed more firmly. "I don't know what I shall do if anything happens to Paul. I just don't know."

"Nothing will happen to Paul," Roger said. "There isn't the slightest reason why it should."

She didn't turn round.

"But he's been so strange."

"It's been a shock."

"It's more than a week now. He ought to have got over it."

"It's bound to take time."

She turned round, suddenly – so suddenly that he couldn't get away. She banged against him, but hardly seemed to notice it. Her face was very close to his, her body, too; and her eyes were glittering, as if she had a fever. Words spilled out, as her lips moved with strange baffling intricacy and speed.

"I feel I've failed him. I ought to have helped him more. I ought to have made him feel that everything was going to work out all right. But I couldn't do it – not with Paul. Rose believed me, and so did little Michael, but Paul – he *knew* how terribly worried I am. He knew from the very first. Where is he? Where has he gone? Don't let anything happen to him. Please, *please,* don't let anything happen to my son."

Roger eased away a little while she spoke. He took her hands, which were trembling with her passionate fears, and her self-blame. Her fingers were icy.

"Before I left my office, I sent a general call out to all police in London," he told her. "They are all on the lookout for him. If I had to guess – and I've two boys of my own, to base a guess on—"

He broke off, deliberately trying to force her to ask what he would say if he had to guess. She was staring at him with burning intensity; and still quivering. It was as if she had stored up all the shock, the fear and the dread while the children had been here, and now it burst out like a flood, the gates opened by this new fear for her son.

"What would you guess? Tell me! *What would you guess?*"

"I would say that young Paul is desperately unhappy because he can't help you," Roger said. "I would think that above everything else, that's what he wants to do."

Was there a little fading of the fire in her eyes?

"Do you—do you really think so?"

"It seems to me what Paul would feel."

"You might be right," she said. She did not take her hands away, but actually drew a little nearer, as if she were afraid that he would let her go but did not want him to. "I don't know. Ever since this morning—but he didn't hear, he couldn't have heard."

"What couldn't he have heard?" asked Roger gently.

"The—the doctor came to see me," she said. Now her voice was steady and small – and touched with a chill which seemed to affect Roger, too; he was almost afraid of what he was going to hear. "Dr Whittaker. Our—our doctor. He had—had a long talk with the surgeon. Semple—Semple-Smith." Now there was no mistaking the fact that the flame of fear in her had been chilled by some new, greater, awful fear. "He was very good—to come. He told me that— he told me—"

She couldn't say it; and as Roger stood there, waiting, gripping her hands tightly, he knew what it was she couldn't say, and a furious rage built up in him against the doctor.

"He told me that Paul might be—be simple. *Simple.* That he might never be the same again. Oh, God, it's awful, it's awful!"

The bloody, bloody, bloody *fool*! Roger thought savagely.

"What am I going to do?" Isobel Bennison cried. Her voice quivered with the chill of that deepest fear. "I haven't been able to think since I heard. I just haven't been able to think. I can't tell anybody. I can't tell neighbours that—that Paul's going to be an idiot. I can't tell the children. How can I?" She did not want an answer, she simply wanted someone who would listen, someone who might even understand. "I've been alone all day. I was glad Paul was out, I didn't feel I could talk to anyone. I've just sat here—all day, I tell you. It wasn't until this evening that I realised he hadn't been to the Oval. I happened to look out of the window, and saw Meg Abbott's children back. I went to find out what had kept Paul, and they told me he hadn't turned up at all. I telephoned you, right away. I *had* to telephone you."

"Of course you did. And everything, everything possible will be done to find Paul." Roger gulped. "Do you seriously think he might have overheard what the doctor said?"

"Yes," she answered, huskily. "We were in the front room. I was so surprised to see Dr Whittaker. I was afraid it was bad news. I didn't say much to Paul, just told him to stay out here, but – the door wasn't quite shut. He might have been in the hall, he might have heard everything. He was so strange this morning, but then he's been strange ever since this happened."

She closed her eyes as if she wanted to shut out some awful dread.

"What am I going to do if my husband *does* become an idiot? What am I going to do?"

Then, quite suddenly, she fell forward as if all the strength had gone out of her legs. She fell against Roger. He held her steady for a few seconds, but she was a dead weight; he thought at first that she had fainted. Gradually, he eased her upright, but still supported her. She was huddled in his arms, hands together in an attitude of prayer and against his chest, very close, helpless, quivering – so she hadn't fainted. He found himself stroking her hair. He found himself pressing her a little closer. He found his face against her hair.

They stood like that for a long time.

Very slowly, the quivering of her body stopped, until she was almost still, but she made no attempt to free herself.

He felt, strangely, remotely, as if he was standing with Janet in his arms, not another woman. There was something right and natural about their closeness; a sense of inevitability. But for her hair, so fair, so golden-coloured, she might have been Janet. The complete surrender of her body, the complete dependence that she had on him for those few minutes, took away all sense of strangeness and brought them together in a union of understanding.

Slowly, she raised her head, but Roger did not take his hand away, only held it there lightly. She reminded him even more of Janet – as Janet had been after Martin-called-Scoop had been taken away by men whom they knew were killers. Janet had screamed and raged and raved at him for "letting it happen" – and then she had collapsed into his arms.

Tears had streaked Isobel Bennison's face, had dimmed her eyes.

"You will help me, won't you?" she begged. "You will help me?"

"I'll help you," he promised.

He must stand back, must take his hand and arms away, must -

"I feel so helpless on my own," she said.

They stood without moving, for what might have been a long time; and then the telephone bell rang.

Chapter Thirteen

Young Paul

The telephone was in the hall – in almost the same position as it was at home. Roger felt the jarring through his head, the note was so harsh and loud. He felt Isobel's body shudder, too – and then her head seemed to move back, but she didn't let him go.

"That might be—"

"I'll answer it," Roger said.

He freed himself, gently. The bell kept ringing, he had never noticed one as harsh and loud as this. *Brrrk-brrrk-brrrk.* He thrust the door back and strode towards the telephone. He stood with his back to the kitchen door, knowing that Isobel was staring at him as he snatched the receiver off.

"This is Mrs Bennison's house."

A woman said: "Is Mrs Bennison -?" and broke off.

Through the mists of his mind, through the strangeness of the last five minutes, the truth came to Roger, and he could hardly believe it. *This was Janet.* It was as if Janet herself was behind him, and yet now was at the other end of the telephone. He shifted his position, and saw that Isobel had come as far as the doorway; some strange compulsion had made him look and make sure that she wasn't Janet. What the hell was happening to him?

"Who is that?" Janet asked, quickly.

"Jan," Roger said. He tried to infuse surprise and heartiness into his voice. Janet would be as startled at finding him here as he was at hearing her. He could see Isobel, now. "It's all right," he called to her.

"Roger," Janet said, at the same moment. "*Is* that you?"

"Yes, darling. I—" he wanted to reassure her, laughingly, or tease her about mistaking his voice, but he couldn't laugh or tease at this moment. "It's a bad line," he said. "How did you know I was here?" The question itself was absurd. She could have called the office; Cope might still be there, and in any case would have left word with the night duty staff so that anyone who called would be able to find him at short notice. He wondered if Janet noticed how oddly he was talking.

"I didn't know," Janet said. "But thank goodness you are. Darling, Paul – young Paul Bennison's here."

Roger stood very still without speaking for several moments, taking in that news. Then he raised his right hand, the thumb cocked, and smiled at Isobel. He saw her as she moved forward again, a smile touching her face with momentary radiance.

"It's all right," he said as she drew nearer. "He's at my home." He looked away from Isobel and spoke into the receiver. "Mrs Bennison was absolutely distraught with worry—you can imagine."

"Yes, I can imagine," Janet said, matter-of-factly. "Roger, he came to—can *she* hear?"

"No."

"He's been wandering about all day, not knowing what to do. Apparently he overheard what the doctor said to his mother this morning. He'd heard you lived in Chelsea, and looked in the telephone directory. He says you're the only one who might be able to help him. He seems to think that everything might work out if you catch the man who attacked his father. He's a bundle of nerves and contradictions and fears. Roger, *is* it really certain, now? I mean, the—the effect on Bennison."

"I haven't been told," Roger said.

Isobel had crept up and was standing very close to him, as if she wanted to hear what was being said. There wasn't much room. He shifted his position, and folded his right arm across his chest, rather than slide it round her waist.

"How *is* Mrs Bennison?" Janet inquired.

"Much better now," said Roger. "She's standing right by me. Would you like a word with her?"

"Yes, of course."

"No," protested Isobel. "No, I don't want to make a fool of myself. I—"

Roger took her hand, placed the telephone receiver in it, and made her lift it to her ear. She was half crying, but that didn't matter – no one else in the world would be able to help her in the way that Janet could; Janet had a gift for dealing with a crisis of this kind. He heard Isobel say something about being silly but she'd been so worried, as he reached the front door. He wanted a drink – he *needed* one. There was a flask in the dashboard pocket. He opened the front door, left it ajar, and strolled to his car.

A man was standing near it.

"Detective Sergeant Robson, sir—from the Division. I'm afraid there's no news of the Bennison boy."

"I've just had some," Roger said. "He turned up at my place, for some odd reason." He hoped that his voice sounded casual enough.

"Oh, that's good, sir!"

"Yes. Use my car radio and tell the Yard, will you? And have them cancel the call to all Divisions. Any other news?"

"I don't think so, sir."

"Other news" of course would mean the capture of Marriott and Dorris. It was strange how completely that had faded from his mind in the last half hour. It was like a problem which belonged to a different world, which someone else had to solve.

He lit a cigarette. The whisky flask could stay in the dashboard pocket – if he took a swig now, the report that Handsome West was on the bottle would go round the Division, and soon the whole of London, like a gust of wind. He strolled back to the house. The door had swung open, and light streamed through. Isobel was still at the telephone, talking more animatedly.

A door opened at the next house, and a middle-aged woman appeared in another stream of light; he recognised her as one of the two whom he had seen on his first visit here.

"Excuse me, are you a police—oh, it's Superintendent West!" She was at her gate.

"Good evening, Mrs Abbott," Roger said. "We've just heard that young Paul is all right."

"Oh, thank goodness for that! We've been so worried. I didn't want to frighten Isobel, but ..." Mrs Abbott went on talking, until the detective came from the car and Isobel came hurrying from her house. "Isobel, I'm *so* relieved ..."

"Yes, Meg, isn't it wonderful? Mr West, your wife said you wouldn't mind taking me to Paul, and if you would I would be most grateful."

"Of course," Roger said. "Finished with the radio, sergeant?"

"Yes, sir."

"Close the front door of the house, and—"

"Isobel, you ought to have a coat, or something round you," said Mrs Abbott.

"Oh, it doesn't matter. I—" Isobel stopped suddenly, put a hand to her hair, and seemed to realise what kind of a mess she must look. Hastily, she turned round. "Yes, of course, I won't be a minute, Mr West. I'll see to the doors." She went hurrying, moving very gracefully despite her mood, and disappeared into the house. Two big moths fluttered near her head.

"The place will be full of moths if she doesn't close that door," Mrs Abbott fussed.

"I'll close it," Roger said.

"You're very kind. I can't tell you what a relief this is – if anything had happened to young Paul on top of what's happened already, I think it would have driven her out of her mind. I must go and tell Mrs Hargreaves that Paul's all right." The friendly neighbour hesitated, then unexpectedly held out her hand. "Mr West, I want to thank you *very* much for all you've done."

"*I've* done nothing!"

"You have, you know," declared Mrs Abbott. "You've made Isobel Bennison and a lot of other people realise that the police care about what happens—really *care*." She began to mumble, squeezed his hand, and hurried along the street.

Roger stood in the hall of the Bennison house, the front door closed against the insects of the night. Now and again he heard movement above – much as he would at home if he were ready to go out, and was waiting for Janet. There were quick, hurried footsteps, and long pauses. He still wanted a drink, but no longer needed it – and in any case wouldn't have one before driving. He was getting back to normal. He smiled grimly to himself, and went in the front room, putting the light on. He remembered the family photograph – the original of one which had been reproduced in the newspapers. Bennison had a fine, strong face; his wife looked younger here, and a happy woman.

She came hurrying down the stairs, and Roger went to the passage door. For a moment, he was completely taken aback, for those few minutes had changed her so much. She had made up, and put on a hat – a small white one, which suited her. And she had changed into a two-piece suit, of dark green – it looked smart, even expensive. Her eyes were brighter, and she had managed to get rid of most of the traces of tears.

"My word," he exclaimed. "That was a quick change!"

"I couldn't go out looking such a mess," she said. "And your wife was so kind." She looked at him, perhaps a little strangely. He stood aside for her to go out, checked that the door latch clicked home, and found the sergeant at the car door, opening it for Isobel. Roger took the wheel. It was the second time he had driven her.

"Goodnight, Robson."

"Goodnight, sir."

Roger eased off the clutch and nosed the car forward. He was aware of faint perfume, from a powder which was not unfamiliar. In the faint light from the dashboard he saw Isobel Bennison's legs stretched out. The skirt cut half-way across her knees. She sat back, as if quite relaxed. When they had turned the comer, she said:

"I quite forgot—I meant to offer you a drink."

"I nearly helped myself," he said, "and then realised that I shouldn't, just before driving. I'm very glad it's worked out like this with young Paul."

"It's a strange thing, but I feel better than I have for a long time," she said. "It's partly because my son's all right, of course, that was such a relief, but—" she hesitated while he passed a slow-moving mini-car, and went on: "But it was mostly because I was able to talk about it to you. I shall never be able to say how much I appreciate—"

"Forget it," Roger said, gruffly.

"I certainly shall not forget it. I shall always be grateful."

"I shall always be glad I could help."

After a pause, she said: "Yes, I believe you will." They were silent for a few seconds, until Roger took out cigarettes and handed the case to her. "I don't smoke, thank you," she said. "My husband and I made a pledge not to, until the mortgage was cleared off the house. We've only three more years to go, and then we shall have a tobacco orgy. We—"

She caught her breath.

"The one thing you've got to remember is that surgeons can be as wrong as anyone," Roger said. "Semple-Smith was only warning the doctor in case something like it happened. He wasn't saying that it's a certainty, no doctor or surgeon could possibly say that."

"Had he told you before?"

"He'd said it was a possibility," Roger answered. "But I'm a long way from convinced that he's right. I'm afraid your husband is going to have a rough time with his leg and his shoulder, but—"

She interrupted.

"Whatever happens I shall have to make the best of it. I'm sure I can." And after a pause, she went on: "I can't tell you how much calmer I feel."

"That's good," Roger said. "That's wonderful."

The light was on in the front room of Roger's Bell Street house when he pulled up, but he could see only Janet in there; not young Paul. He helped Isobel out of the car, and they walked to the front door. Janet opened the door as they reached it, eager and glad to see them. Her hands went out to Isobel, woman-to-woman.

"Don't talk too loud," she said to Roger. "They're in the living room with the television on. Thank heavens there was a Western tonight!" She led the way into the front room, almost conspiratorially, and Roger glanced round and thought: *Bless your heart.* For a supper table was laid, with sandwiches, biscuits, slices of melon and some apples and bananas. Coffee and tea were at hand, a kettle was plugged into the point by the fireplace.

"Paul was ravenous," Janet went on. "And he said he didn't think you'd been eating much lately, either. *Do* sit down." If she noticed the tears in Isobel's eyes, she ignored them. "The Western goes on until ten past ten, so we've still twenty minutes. Would you like tea or coffee, Mrs Bennison?"

"Or a real drink?" suggested Roger.

"I'd love some coffee."

"Then I'll have the drink," Roger said, and turned to the sideboard where they kept the store of sherry, gin and whisky with all the accessories, and helped himself to the whisky and soda he had been wanting for an hour.

The two women sat down. There wasn't really much likeness between them, except – well, Janet's hair *was* rather thick and naturally wavy and cut in the same fashion, although so dark except where there were touches of grey; facially they could hardly have been more different, but their figures …

"Please *do* help yourself," Janet said.

"Now that's an idea," murmured Roger, reaching forward. Isobel smiled up at him, brushed a hand across her eyes, and took a sandwich. "What did happen?"

"Paul arrived here about half an hour before I telephoned you, and asked to see you," Janet explained. "I recognised him from the newspapers, and I could see that he seemed upset. He wouldn't talk to me, but Scoop and Fish were in, and I left him with them. One or the other made him start talking, and once started he couldn't stop. I *think* he was really suffering from a kind of delayed shock. The thing which worried him most was that he couldn't think of a way to help you, Mrs Bennison, and—"

"Isobel," murmured Roger.

"Eh? Oh, of course," Janet gave a natural little laugh. "Yes, that's much more friendly. What was I saying? Oh, yes. As far as Scoop could make out, Paul felt that if my husband could catch the men who were responsible you could all make a fresh start. I think that's become a kind of fixation with him. When *are* you going to catch them, darling?"

Roger shrugged: "The first moment we can."

"Did Paul say much about—about this morning and the doctor's visit?" asked Isobel, very quietly.

"Not much. As a matter of fact, I think Richard did him a lot of good. He told Richard about this—suggestion of—"

"Mental shock," interpolated Isobel.

Janet said levelly: "Yes, that's the phrase Paul used. Richard's reaction was to jump up and say that all doctors were probably a bit mad, anyhow, like all school teachers. It made Paul laugh."

"I think the West family has a kind of magic wand," Isobel said. She was eating the sandwiches with a steadiness which was a good sign in itself. "I was at my wits' end when your husband came." Two sandwiches later, Isobel asked: "Do you think your boys could possibly persuade Paul to go and spend the rest of the week with his grandparents? I think I would be better on my own."

"What I was going to suggest was that he should go with Scoop and Richard to camp this week-end," said Janet. "They're going for four week-ends altogether, and next week is the third one and the longest—Thursday to Tuesday. It's a school camp, but friends are allowed, and it's not expensive. Do you think that would be all right?"

"If only Paul will go," Isobel said.

"I like your Mrs Bennison," Janet said, when she and Roger were in bed together, a little before midnight. "When *are* you going to find these men, darling?"

"You have the same feeling as young Paul, have you?"

"In a way I suppose I have. I think they'll all feel that they're off to a fresh start."

"I know what you mean," Roger said gruffly. "If that doctor hadn't—"

"I don't know that he was wrong, except in not making sure that the boy didn't hear—and perhaps in telling her without seeing that a woman or friends were with her. Supposing she had felt that her husband was getting better physically, and then suddenly found out there was something the matter with his mind. That shock would have been worse, surely."

"I wonder," said Roger.

They did not talk much more, and soon dropped off to sleep, Roger's last thought being of his absurd feeling that Isobel Bennison *had* been Janet. That had faded when he woke next morning, late enough to be in a hurry.

He reached the office before nine o'clock, hoping that there would be news, and found Cope on the telephone, talking eagerly, his eyes lighting up when Roger went in. Cope cocked a thumb. Roger said: *"Have we got 'em?"* and felt like snatching the receiver away from his assistant.

"… yes, he's here right now. I'll tell him." Cope banged down the receiver, pushed his chair back and bumped his head against the wall, but took no notice of it. "Handsome, they've got Dorris's and Marriott's bodies ! They were found in the Thames near Greenwich an hour ago. It looks as if …"

Chapter Fourteen

Plot

Simister looked up from the grisly objects on the bench, adjusted his glasses, and wrinkled his nose. It was in the middle of the afternoon.

"There is no sign of injury or any bruising, no sign at all that they were held under water. The water in the lungs is identical in all respects to the water from that stretch of the Thames – I've had the analysis checked and double-checked. There is a little oil, a little faeces as usual from the ships, a few specks of sawdust, some ..."

"It looks to me as if they fixed up a passage on one of the ships, probably the *Glambia*, and couldn't make it," Cope said later. "Too greedy – if they hadn't clipped that gold inside their clothes they might have got ashore. The boat was picked up at low tide. It was an old leaky dinghy which was stolen from Hill's Wharf. There was a hole in it, which could be plugged with cork."

"Any hope of getting hold of that cork?" asked Roger.

"Shouldn't think so," Cope said.

Roger was scraping the surface of one of the "gold" belts, with his pen-knife, and as he spoke, the bright shimmer of gold showed through the dull grey of lead. Cope jumped up.

"That's phoney!" he exclaimed. "Lead with a thin layer of gold. See that?"

"I see it," Roger said grimly. "It's an old, popular racket—lascars get caught by it time and time again. The question is, did Dorris and Marriott know it was lead?"

"Or were they sold a pup? If so, who did it?"

"One more thing to find out," Roger reasoned. "We'd better try to trace where these came from."

He knew that the task would be nearly impossible, but it had to be attempted.

The Press splashed the news next morning, taking it for granted that Dorris and Marriott had died while trying to escape from the police net.

The inquest verdict was "Accidental Death".

No one else seemed to have the slightest suspicion of foul play, and Roger kept his own suspicion to himself.

Campbell, now back to the normal place of second-in-command, for the Commander was home from his holiday, still served as liaison between the executive and the administrative branches. After Roger had got back from the inquest, he came breezing into the office, a tall, rangy, fair-haired man who moved rather as if he were double-jointed.

"The Old Man's a bit sour," he reported. "Especially as he's going off for three weeks to Italy—he wanted a clear mind for his holiday. The Home Secretary's got to go to Geneva too. The pressure's off, Handsome."

Roger didn't speak.

"Any line on the two men who are still missing?" inquired Campbell.

"No," Roger said.

Until he found them, he would not have a moment's real peace – and although one pressure was eased, others were tight about him. Bennison had regained consciousness on the day that the bodies had been taken out of the Thames, but had not recognised his wife, and had not spoken an intelligible word. He lay there, looking vacant, almost as if he could not see. Then he relapsed into unconsciousness.

The one real cause for relief was that young Paul seemed to be much nearer normal. He was often at Bell Street, and occasionally Roger's boys went over to Wimbledon with him. There had been at least two family tea parties during the week, when Roger couldn't be present.

"I think the truth is that Isobel is refusing to admit the possibility of the worst happening," Janet reported. "She's closing her mind to it."

"Could be." Roger was non-committal.

"You're still worried about the case, aren't you?" Janet said, and when he didn't answer, she went on quietly but with obvious certainty that she was right: "You haven't been yourself since it happened, darling. You've taken it too much to heart. You ought to know by now that when Isobel asked you why you let it happen, she didn't mean it. Not personally. She was distraught."

"I know," Roger said. He thought: *Haven't I been myself?* What was the difference, that Janet should notice it?

"What really is worrying you?" Janet asked.

He said, slowly, heavily, deliberately clouding the issue:

"Two out of four of that gang are still at large. They might strike again. I suppose I'll be a bit preoccupied until they're caught."

"That is all, isn't it?" asked Janet.

"Yes," he said. "Of course."

"There isn't anything else worrying you, at the Yard? No other case—?"

He made himself laugh, made himself throw his arms round her, and hug her until she protested, breathlessly; and he made himself kiss her full on the lips.

The almost unbelievable, unbearable thing was that he *had* to make himself.

Afterwards, he thought: "I've got to get those two men. I won't get this job out of my system until I have." He studied all the reports on the case again, closely, and always came back to one question: *why* had Charley Blake been murdered with that one, swift, merciless stab?

Blake had been a sailor; Dorris had been a docker. Was there any significance in that?

So far, he could see none.

Two weeks after the murders of Dorris and Marriott, Steve Stevens and Alec Gool met, as if by chance, at Stamford Bridge. The football season was now two weeks old. Chelsea had won two games in dazzling fashion, home and away, and lost another by a display of such ineptitude that the crowds on the terraces were tonight prepared to jeer. Steve had bought the tickets. They sat together in a corner of the main stand, with empty seats all around them. It was a golden evening, the sun shone out of a cloudless sky, the temperature was in the seventies, crowd as well as players were sweating. The blue jerseys and the red jerseys and the light ball made gay swift-moving patterns on grass unbelievably green after a few days of rain.

"Nothing's happened for this long, and nothing's likely to," Alec Gool said. "No reason why we shouldn't be seen around together now, Steve."

"Maybe not," said Steve. He watched the Chelsea outside right push the ball past the prancing back and dart after it. "But we'd better keep to ourselves for a bit longer."

"Steve," said Alec Gool. "What's the real reason?"

The outside left ballooned the ball over the bar.

"What's that?"

"What's the real reason?"

"I don't know what you're talking about."

"You have plenty of time to hang around the Hornpipe, but I'm not supposed to be there at the same time. I like that pub. I always have."

"One of these days you can go back there," said Steve. He turned to look at the youth, his eyes very hard and very narrow. "Don't start work on anything that isn't your business, son."

"My business is making sure we don't run into trouble," Alec retorted, "and I'm going to do it. You shouldn't spend so much time with that *widow.*"

"Alec—" Steve's right hand fastened on the other's knee and he gripped tightly, increasing the pressure, knowing he was causing a lot of pain. Gool took no notice, and watched the field as the ball swept towards the other end. "I'm warning you."

"Steve," said Gool softly. "Maybe you've forgotten that you might talk in your sleep." The pressure relaxed. "And Joyce Conway's got a conscience – don't make any mistake about that. She's got what they call a social conscience. She's the kind who always believes in telling the truth no matter how much it hurts you. Isn't she, Steve?"

"So," Steve said.

"If she ever found out—"

"She won't."

"Don't you ever talk in your sleep?"

"Alec," Steve said, glancing round and making sure that no one could possibly be within earshot, "you can start thinking about other things. Take your choice, but don't get under my skin while you're doing it. That could get you into a lot of trouble. And remember this: one of these days one of the people who saw you driving that lorry or saw me at Covent Garden is going to see us again. It's bound to happen." When Alec made no comment, just watched the weaving figures on the field, hearing the occasional roar or shout of advice and the thwacking sound of boot on ball, Steve went on: "London's no place for us now."

"Then where is?"

"I could name a hundred places, but not London—not for a long time."

"If you're going to run away, why haven't you -?"

"Alec," said the older man, "I didn't cut and run for one good reason. Money. It's no use running when you're broke. New York or Buenos Aires, Sydney or Cape Town, Paris or Moscow—you need money in them all. Plenty of money. But we couldn't pull off another job while the police were still looking for us. We know there were good descriptions of the other two—we don't know there aren't any descriptions of us."

He stopped.

"Now you're making sense," Alec Gool said. His eyes were much brighter, although he shaded them with his hand against the bright sunlight on the green. "I thought—"

"You thought that I was staying in London because of my lady friend. That isn't the first mistake you've made, and you'll make a lot more. I stayed because it was the safest place. Once we run we are likely to be noticed. While if I lead a normal life people will take less notice of me, won't they?"

Alec drew in a deep breath.

"My God," he said, "you're smart. You've been using her!"

"That's a way to put it," said Steve. "Now, listen, son. We stay away from each other except after dark, or in crowds. We don't do that because of the Covent Garden job—we do it because when we pull the next job, the big one, we don't want anyone to be able to say that they've seen us together. Got that?"

"I've got it. What job is it going to be?"

"When I'm ready for it, I'll tell you," Steve said. "Your job is to obtain passports in different names, and get us certificates, also in different names. Pay a bit on account and the rest later—like you bought your scooter. We want to pull off one big job and be ready to flit after it. The opportunity might come next week, or it might come in a month's time. Get those passports and papers ready."

"I can fix it," Alec said.

"Sure?"

"You don't have to worry."

"Then I won't worry," said Steve. "I want those papers next Monday evening—at the Fulham match. Same time—and I'll have tickets. I'll slip yours to you outside the E turnstile for the stands, and we'll meet inside. That clear?"

"I've got it," Alec said. For a while they watched the game, and for a while it was worth watching – until a man in blue shot yards wide from close in, and a groan from the crowd swelled up into a howl of derision. Suddenly, Alec said: "Steve, you got any idea what it will be?"

"Just forget it," Steve said.

"I've got a right to know."

"When you bring me those passports and my second mate's certificate in a different name, you'll have a right to know. Until then you don't have any rights with me."

"Okay, okay," said Alec, as if he were satisfied. "I'll see you Monday."

It was not surprising, although it was sheer chance, that two guards who regularly escorted the wages officers of a large manufacturing company on the Great West Road, were watching the match that evening. It was not even surprising that one of the wages officers was there, too. The second wages officer was at home, at his Hounslow house; gardening.

The more she thought about Steve, the less Joyce Conway felt that she understood him. But the more she saw of him, the greater her love for him became. Deep down, she had a sense of fear, almost of premonition, that it could not and would not last. Whenever she let herself think about this – usually after she had lulled herself into dreaming of false hopes of marriage – she put this down to the fact that he was a sailor, and that one day the sea would lure him away again. So far, he showed no sign of wanting to go.

He did not spend every night with her.

She was never sure when he would want to come, never sure even when he would come to the Hornpipe, but he had a remarkable gift for taking her by surprise. The night when she felt certain he would not come, it being so near closing time, would find him waiting at the corner. The night she felt sure he would come in for a drink, he did not show up. The night when she was resigned to a weary two or three hours in the pub, was the night when he would be the first to push open the door.

He always looked the same, clean-cut, distinguished, sardonic. She knew that he was much cleverer than she was, that her simplicity amused him, but that didn't matter. He seemed to be in love with her. Most of the time she refused to believe that this was a love that would not last.

Sometimes, when he came home with her, he raised her to a state of quivering ecstasy which seemed to be the very purpose of life itself. He was so gentle when gentleness was needed, so masterful and possessive, yet so willing to surrender.

Now and again, she wished he would talk more about himself, but she had the sense not to ask him. A little of his past came out at odd moments, and she began to build up a picture of a life spent travelling round the world, fighting, adventuring; there was a glow of romance about him which she built up into an even greater image.

On the Monday after the match at Chelsea – she knew he had been there – she was leaving the pub after lunch, at about a quarter past three, when she saw Alec Gool. He was coming out of a jobbing printer's who had a couple of presses in a shed behind the tiny shop where he sold stationery and cigarettes. Alec grinned at her, and touched his forehead – an obsequiousness which she knew was a form of derision. She had never liked him. As she walked on, she wondered why he had behaved like that, it was as if he were simply taking the mickey out of her.

She glanced round from the corner, but he wasn't looking back.

As he reached the far corner, however, she saw a very attractive, long-legged girl from a hairdresser's come out and look at him. As far as Joyce could see, Gool did not even glance at her. Most youths of his age would have stopped to have a word, or at the very least looked her up and down – and they would have looked back, too. Gool didn't. He was queer all right.

Joyce suddenly remembered thinking that Steve shouldn't have much to do with him – and now the thought that Steve might be associated with a "queer" struck her as so funny that she laughed aloud.

She let herself into the tiny home.

It was spick and span, as always; and she had taken even more trouble since the *affaire* with Steve. On her small dressing-table were two bottles of expensive make-up – of a kind she had only seen advertised – which Steve had given her; he could be very generous. On the bedside table were some books, Penguins, by authors she had never heard of. Steve seemed to like them, but whenever she tried to read a page or two, she was bored stiff – but then, reading had never attracted her. The fact that there was a man about the house was obvious – his silver-backed hair-brush, which she had bought him, for instance. Two or three ties were rolled round to get the creases out, and on the dressing-table, not in a drawer; she liked to see them about. In the kitchen the tea tray was always set with two cups and saucers these days, one of them a breakfast cup – whether tea or coffee, he liked a man's quantity.

She wished she had a photograph of him, but had never suggested it. Deep down, there was a fear of what would happen if she did.

She had left home before looking at the newspapers, which usually arrived about half-past nine. Steve had been here, and hadn't left until just before she had. She had had a pork pie and a shandy at the pub, part of her perquisites. Now she put her legs up on the bed, switched on the radio for music and picked up the newspapers. She thumbed the *Mirror* through idly, and soon came to an inside page which had pictures – not photographs – of two men on it, and two smaller photographs below. The heading was:

DO YOU KNOW THESE MEN?

These are composite pictures of two men wanted for questioning by the police about the murder of Charley Blake, a wages guard, in Covent Garden last month.

The bodies of two men known to have taken part in the raid were found in the Thames two weeks ago, as the *Mirror* reported at the time. The two men shown here were probably in the company of the two drowned men, whose photographs are below, at the time of the murder.

The photograph of Win Marriott was a very good one; she had known but never liked him. Even as a schoolboy, he had been big-headed and big-mouthed. She hardly knew the boxer, Dorris, although she had heard of him, and had seen him occasionally.

She had a feeling that she had seen one of the men in the composite pictures before – one who looked young. She pondered this for a few minutes, glancing out of the window and trying to call him to mind. Soon she gave up. It was none of her business, and even if she did remember anything, and told the police, it would lead to a lot of trouble and bother – it wasn't as if she would be able to say for sure who he was.

Who *did* he remind her of?

The question teased her at odd moments, while she listened to *Music While You Work*, finished the papers, then went into the kitchen and made herself some tea. She felt refreshed, and had tea while ironing a slip and some panties, and also a shirt for Steve. One of the things she liked about Steve was his fastidiousness over clothes; he didn't like wearing the same shirt for more than two days, and told her that one day for one pair of socks was the most any man should allow.

Who *was* that drawing like? Someone she knew, someone she had seen recently. It was like a name on the tip of her tongue. Who—?

Gracious!

It reminded her of Alec Gool.

Chapter Fifteen

Sanity

Alec Gool sidled along the empty benches in a corner of the grand stand at the Fulham Football Club's ground, towards Steve, who was sitting by himself, hand on his chin, watching the players kick the ball about at the beginning of the game. The evening was dull and drab. Even the white of the Fulham players' shirts looked greyish. The terraces were no more than half full, especially on the side which backed on to the river. The Thames was in flood, and the tops of sails showed as small yachts tacked up and down.

Alec sat down as the referee's whistle blew, and he beckoned the two captains. The visitor tossed the coin. As Johnny Haynes moved his arm to show which way Fulham would kick, there was a cheer of satisfaction from the crowd.

"Well?" said Steve.

"I've got them," Alec said. "And they're beauties."

"Got them with you?"

"In an envelope—want to see them?"

"Hand 'em over."

Steve glanced round casually. A man and two small boys were hurrying along the seats just below, nearer than he wanted anyone to be; then they clattered down a gangway, safely out of range. Steve took a buff-coloured envelope, opened it, and took out a passport. He felt it, rubbed his thumb over the mottled dark surface, smiled tautly with satisfaction and opened it. His own picture looked up at him – a poor one, taken at one of the photograph machines in a fun fair, but quite recognisable. The details were his, exactly – height, weight, colour of hair, colour of eyes, no distinguishing marks – but the name was Bennett; Joseph Bennett.

"Okay, Steve?" Gool was eager for praise.

"Looks all right."

Steve was about to unfold a certificate when there was a roar from the crowd, followed by a surge of people to their feet and another, greater, roar. *"Goal!"* The two boys who had just come in were cheering wildly, half-a-dozen players in white were mobbing another, while players in red were trooping back towards the centre line, as if glumly.

Not far away, standing at one of the entrances to the stand, was Cope, Roger West's second-in-command. Cope was clapping, but looking about him. He was first and last a policeman, and one of the reasons for being here was to watch for pick-pockets among the crowd. As the goal was scored, he let out a bellow of satisfaction, then looked about quickly. Anyone not roaring his head off or looking glum was suspect. The two men sitting half way down the stand, near one side, were not really taking any interest; he saw them glance up, and saw one of them open a paper which did not look like a pools entry form. It might be a match programme. Cope made a mental note to look at them from time to time, and watched the players in red kick off.

Unaware of this scrutiny, Steve Stevens looked down at a forged mate's certificate, also made out in the name of Joseph Bennett. As far as he could judge, it was perfect. It was – or it looked – an old one, and had several official stamps on it.

"Okay, Steve?" Gool repeated.

"You'll do."

"Got anything planned yet?"

"Yes."

"That's what I wanted to hear. When and where?"

"Wednesday. Linstone's, Great West Road. Worth ten thousand quid. We don't do it at the bank, we do it at the factory. You're going to work there, Alec."

"What's work?"

"They need packers," announced Steve. "So you can pack. The wages office is near the small goods warehouse where they need the packers. I know—I worked there once."

"Holding out on me, eh?"

"That's not so hard. There's a strong guard—Linstone men, police and a couple of bank guards up to the moment they bring the money into the factory. Once it's inside, they stop worrying. It's taken into the wages office. There's one guard inside and another outside the room, all the time the wages staff are making up the wage packets. The time for us is just after the money's in the office and before they start splitting it up."

Alec glanced at him.

There was a shout from the crowd: *"Get rid of it!"* Alec turned away from Steve and watched the game, still without speaking. Further off, Cope looked down and saw that the younger of the two men was now intent on the game: that looked all right. The older was putting the paper back into his pocket. Why were they sitting on their own? Why didn't they go down the stand, where there were plenty of empty seats, so that they could get a better view?

"Steve," Alec said.

"Well?"

"We're inside the factory. How do we get outside?"

"I'm coming to collect some spare parts for a Stepney garage. In a plain van. That money is put on a truck to wheel into the wages office—didn't I tell you? I'm in the warehouse, waiting for the order. You're packing in the same warehouse. We know the right moment to strike because they put a factory guard at the door leading from the warehouse to the offices. He's in uniform."

Alec was still watching the play – Haynes was weaving, a man in red shoulder-charged him.

"Foul!"

"Dirty work, ref. *Ref!* How about that?"

Haynes went after the man with the ball.

"There are two of us," Alec said. "Just two. We agreed on that."

"Right."

"And how many of them?"

"Say six or seven. It could be sixteen or seventeen, and it wouldn't make any difference. You'll have tear gas and smoke bombs. I've had some by me for a long time, waiting for the right job. Before the police can get there you and I will have the money truck. There's only one more guard, two wages officers, a bunch of scared girls—and ten thousand quid on a truck."

"It's a hell of a risk."

"Galling it off?" asked Steve, casually.

Alec didn't speak.

"If you are, tell me," Steve said. "If not—go and get that job at Linstone's tomorrow morning. They're so hungry for packers they'd take a deaf mute."

"I'll case the joint," Alec promised.

From then on, they paid more attention to the game. Cope, who had intended to go and take a closer look, was distracted by the sight of a little grey-haired man slipping furtively away down some steps – a man whom he knew as a pick-pocket of experience and exceptional skill. He went after this man, put a hand on his shoulder before he reached the exit, and grinned.

"Lemme go!" The protest was shrill. "I don't feel well, I've got to go home."

"It depends what you call home, Syd," said Cope. "Let's have a look in your pocket."

When he left the ground, Cope felt that he had had a very successful evening; and Fulham had won, three-one.

Roger heard about the arrest of the pick-pocket and the fact that he had had five wallets in his pocket, told Cope how smart he was, and turned his attention to the twenty-seven letters, from all parts of the country, saying that twenty-seven different individuals had seen one or the other originals of the composite drawings in various places at the same time. There was no useful information in any of them. He spent half an hour on the job, then pushed the file away. Cope, still flushed with success, glanced across at him.

"You okay, Handsome?"

"Don't I look it?"

"If you ask me, this Bennison job's got under your skin too deep," said Cope. "Be a good thing if you went off it on to another job. Not that you won't, soon—the V.I.P. pressure is off, and as soon as we have a big job in, you'll get it. How's Janet?"

"Fine."

"Mrs Bennison?"

"Very well, I think."

"What's the latest on Bennison?" inquired Cope.

"He's out of danger," answered Roger. "He still hasn't spoken and they're still not sure what he'll come round like." He did not add that it would not be long before there was some positive indication of what Bennison would be like when he had recovered, physically, as far as possible. He knew that Isobel now went to the hospital for at least half an hour each day. A Yard man was always there on duty, but Roger was wondering whether it was worth keeping him there – it was more and more doubtful whether Bennison would be able to say anything coherently, still less that he would be able to give them any information which might help to find the two men who were still missing.

At two o'clock, there was a call from Winfrifh, at the hospital.

"The nurses say Bennison's likely to come round any time. Thought you would like to know."

Roger's heart missed a beat.

"Thanks," he said. "I'll come and see him myself, right away."

He told himself that his eagerness to go had nothing to do with the fact that Isobel would be there about that time. But it had. Later, he would tell Janet, would say that he had to handle it personally, so everything would be above board. It was so long since he had tried to lie to himself that he felt awkward and uneasy as he went up to the private ward. The card: *Do Not Enter* hung from a hook, so the nurses or a doctor was in there; that lunatic of a G.P.! He waited for a few minutes, then opened the door an inch. He heard a man's voice, and a woman's. At the same moment, foot steps rapped sharply on the corridor. Without turning round, he knew that it was Isobel. He closed the door and turned.

She was very much more herself, for she had rested sufficiently during the past week to bring brightness back to her eyes, and vigour and sprightliness back to her body. She wore a bottle green suit trimmed with black, and it suited her – she dressed very well, with more flair for clothes than Janet. Probably she spent more money on them, too. She smiled at him, brightly – unfeignedly glad to see him.

"Are you locked out?"

"I think a doctor is in there," Roger said. "I'm not sure who—"

He broke off as the door opened and a short, very thickset man with a chunky face and a small red wart on the side of his nose, strode out. He wore a shabby white smock. It was Semple-Smith, and his eyes, almost black, held a glint of excitement.

He stopped short.

"Mrs Bennison, I was told you were likely to come in today. I think your husband may recognise you. If he does that is the most encouraging sign we've had. Will you go in quite normally, go up and sit by the side of the bed, and speak to him—much as you would if you were taking him some tea in bed at home. Be as matter-of-fact as you can."

Isobel's hand clutched Roger's arm.

"Yes. Yes, of course." Her tension was back, so much that it reflected in the sharpness of her voice, and in the way she looked. "Yes," she repeated. She suddenly realised that she was holding Roger's arm, and let him go. "Will you come in with me?"

"I'll stand just inside the door," said Semple-Smith. "I would like you to be alone with him, or as nearly as possible alone." He looked at Roger, and there was something objectionably superior in his manner. "You're West, aren't you? The policeman."

Roger said stiffly: "Yes."

"Can you get your man out of there? He's like a limpet."

"No," said Roger. "I can't. If Mr Bennison is likely to speak this is the very moment we've had a man here for."

"I want him out," Semple-Smith said coldly.

"If you prefer it, I'll take his place."

"It doesn't make any difference who's in there. I won't have Bennison questioned."

Roger sensed Isobel watching him, sensed the irritation and exasperation of the surgeon, fought back an impulse to answer as rudely, and said quietly: "I'll take my man's place, I think. And of course I won't ask any questions – no one will, without your express permission." He moved towards the door, and opened it. Semple-Smith made no attempt to stop him. Winfrith was sitting in a corner, looking a little sheepish. Roger beckoned, and when Winfrith reached the door, said: "I'll take over. Had anything?"

"Just a word."

"Wait for me." Roger stood aside, and Semple-Smith came in, nodded curtly, waited for Roger to take the vacant chair in the corner, partly hidden by a fabric screen. A middle-aged nurse moved the screen a little; Roger could see the man lying there. The pallor was the same, but there were fewer bandages and Bennison looked less top-heavy. His eyes were closed, but he seemed to be breathing more regularly and with more strength. There were whisperings at the door, but Bennison did not look round or open his eyes.

Isobel stepped in. She glanced at Roger, and quickly away. Again he had that strange feeling, that she was so like Janet – that he felt for her much as he would feel for Janet in times of trouble. She looked at her best as she stealthily moved to the side of the bed. A chair was in position. The nurse stood looking over the screen from the wall.

Isobel sat down.

"Hallo, Paul," she said, in a clear voice. "How are you, dear?"

Bennison's eyes flickered. They opened, very slowly. He was facing the ceiling, and continued to stare at it. Blankly. Semple-Smith was breathing heavily through his nose.

"I'm here, Paul," Isobel said. It was easy to sense the effort she made to keep her voice clear and steady. She sat with hands in her lap, staring down at her husband, with fear and anxiety and *hope* in her eyes. Her lips were unsteady, her fingers working.

Bennison turned his head towards the direction of the sound. He stopped. He frowned. Isobel smiled and bent a little closer. In that moment from that angle she was quite beautiful.

"Hallo, darling," she said. "It's me. Bel."

Bennison's lips moved, and he *smiled*. Semple-Smith's right hand descended on Roger's shoulder and gripped – Roger doubted whether he knew what he was doing.

Bennison whispered: *"Bel."* Not Isobel, just the last syllable. He kept smiling. *"Bel"* he repeated. The hand outside the bedspread moved, and Isobel took it gently, her own suddenly quite steady. She was as gentle as Janet when one of the boys was ill.

"Yes, I'm here, Paul."

He seemed to draw in a deep breath, and then spoke quite clearly: "It's good to see you." Pause. "I'm sorry—I've worried you."

"Don't be silly, darling."

"It must have been—terrible."

"We knew you would be all right. It was just a matter of waiting."

"Waiting," he said. "I know. Waiting." He made the word a sigh. "How—how is young Paul?"

"He's fine, darling."

"Fine," echoed Bennison. "And—the others?"

"They're fine, too."

"I'd like to see them."

"You shall, as soon as possible."

"Bel," Bennison said again, and smiled more deeply, the corners of his lips turning down in a way which was almost droll. He seemed to relax, and closed his eyes slowly. After a moment, Isobel leaned forward and put her lips to his forehead. When she drew back, Bennison's hand was very limp in hers, and his eyes were still closed.

"That's enough, he's gone off again," Semple-Smith said, in a hoarse whisper. "He'll be all right, though. Thank God."

Isobel looked up. There were tears in her eyes, and they began to spill over her lashes. Roger remembered when he had last seen her crying and distraught – she wasn't distraught now.

Semple-Smith moved towards her.

"He'll come round again soon. Sure to. Can you stay at the hospital, so that we can have you here in a few minutes whenever he does come round?" When she didn't answer, he went on: "He said 'Bel' when he first came round—said it several times."

"That's all I've got down, sir," said Winfrith. "Bennison kept saying 'Bel'. I've got it down as the ordinary word 'bell'. That's what it sounded like."

"It was good enough," Roger said. "Take your corner again, will you?"

"If the old pig will let me?"

"Semple-Smith?"

"It isn't often I want to tear a strip off a man, but—"

"I know," said Roger. "Don't worry, he'll be all right." He watched Winfrith go into the ward. A moment later Semple-Smith came out, with Isobel. She was trying to smile now. She didn't look at Roger; it was as if he wasn't there.

"... of course I'll stay here for as long as necessary. I can sleep in the ward, if that would help."

"Oh, there's no need for that," said the surgeon. "Just be at hand."

"Will I be able to telephone a neighbour so that my children will be looked after?"

"Of course. From the Sister's office."

"Thank you," Isobel said. She looked at Roger, and although he would never be able to find words for it, he realised that something had happened to her, something had changed her attitude towards him completely. It was almost as if she was looking at a stranger. Her smile was bright but formal. "Isn't it wonderful?" she said. "Wonderful!"

"I am very pleased," Roger said, as formally.

"It's wonderful," she repeated, and dabbed at her eyes. Then she turned to Semple-Smith. "Doctor, there isn't any reason to fear for his mind now, is there?"

"No," Semple-Smith said. "No." They walked along the passage together until they came to the Sister's office. He tapped on the door, the Sister appeared, there was a hurried consultation. Roger walked past. He had a sense of remoteness; a sense almost that an era had passed. It was very, very strange. He reached the top of the stairs, walked down, and blew his nose very hard.

As he passed the reception office, a porter called out:

"Superintendent West?"

"Yes." If this were an urgent call from the Yard it was exactly what he needed.

"Mr Semple-Smith would like you to wait for a few minutes, sir."

"Oh." Here was the surgeon, giving orders again. It was tempting to say that he was in a hurry, but the thought was almost small-minded, Roger decided; he would wait for five minutes, anyhow.

"Can I smoke?"

"Oh, yes, sir. And I'll bring a chair." Physically, Roger was quite comfortable. Mentally, he was disturbed and dismayed – dismayed because the change in Isobel Bennison had stung so much. Where had he been going? How far would he have gone?

He found himself sweating.

"I've got to get a hold on myself," he said in a whisper. "I've got to get things straight. I want the killer, because it's my job. That's all."

He began to think with fierce concentration, and as always on this case, he came back to the question: why had the lean man killed so quickly?

Roger stubbed out a second cigarette. As he did so the surgeon came from another passage, dressed in a navy-blue blazer, light flannel trousers, stamping down with iron-tipped heels; he looked and walked rather like a navvy.

He drew level with Roger.

"Damned good thing up there," he said. "Taught me in future never to breathe a word about this kind of thing to anyone—I ought to be more like a policeman, and keep my thoughts to myself. Well, I'm off home. Had a hell of a morning. Started at half past two trying to save the life of a man who got drunk and drove at a hundred miles an hour. Had three emergencies since then, all heads. Just as I was going off I heard about Bennison. We must have a drink one day. Good afternoon."

He stamped on.

Roger stared after him – and began to smile.

Roger went straight back to the office. Nothing new was in. He took out the files on the Covent Garden case and went through them again in detail. He kept making notes, until gradually his mind cleared and he began to move along one specific line of inquiry.

Why *had* Charley Blake been killed so quickly? With differing degrees of emphasis the eye-witnesses' statements all said the same thing – there had been one swift, savage thrust. Until now, Roger had told himself that the obvious reason was that the killer had meant to take no chances; the whole job had been ruthless. But could the killer and Blake have known each other? It was a guess, but it would fit the statements. Supposing, on the instant of meeting, recognition had shown in one man's eyes? Wouldn't that explain a swift murderous thrust from a ruthless man?

Roger kept working at it, sorted out all the files to do with Blake, Marriott and Dorris, and stuffed them into his brief-case. He left the office at half past five, earlier than usual. For once he had a good run home, in spite of the rush hour. As he pulled into the garage, he heard the clatter of a lawn-mower. He went quietly to the back garden.

Martin was pushing the mower, and looking hot and sticky. Richard was trimming the edges of the lawn. Janet was on her knees at the herbaceous border which ran along one fence. Something made her look up; as she did so, she seemed so young, so eager.

Her eyes lit up.

"Roger!"

"Oh, hallo, Dad." Scoop stopped the machine immediately. "Dad, what about that motor-mower we were talking about?"

"Hi, Dad!" called Richard. "These edging shears want doing something to. What do you think happened today? I beat Simpson at table tennis …"

"I'll bet you couldn't beat me," Roger said.

There was a lilt in his voice, excitement born of emotion which hadn't been in him for a long time. It was as if a great weight had been lifted off his shoulders. He saw Janet's eyes light up again. When he told her what had happened at the hospital, he could tell that she was delighted. He did not think she had the slightest idea that he had been so preoccupied with another woman.

What the hell was the matter with him? He had come very close to making a fool of himself.

One thing was certain, he repeated again; he was going to find Charley Blake's killer simply because he was a copper.

Janet went to bed early.

Roger took the papers out of the brief-case, and sank himself into the reports.

If the killer had recognised Blake, the obvious course was to find out who, among Blake's friends or acquaintances – perhaps fellow seamen – could be described as tall, lean and sharp-featured. He studied the reports which men from the Yard and the Divisions had prepared. The dossier on Blake was remarkably thorough. He had not been to sea for five years. He had worked at four places since then – always as a watchman or a guard.

Roger made a note of the places.

Hoover Ltd. – Western Avenue Wimpey's – building site at Wembley Linstone's, Great West Road – Car accessory and tyre manufacturers

Revel & Son Ltd. – Covent Garden.

"We can cut Revel's out," Roger said musingly. "We'll have a go at the other three."

He knew only too well that it was the kind of job which would probably turn out to be a complete dead-end, but finding Charley Blake's killer was a matter of honour, as well as his job.

"It's okay," Alec Gool said into a telephone. "I've landed the job, it was as easy as you said. Now I've seen the lay-out, there's no trouble. But I've got a suggestion to make, Steve. Or should I call you Joe?"

Steve, standing in the call-box just outside the Hornpipe, said smoothly: "I'm Steve until after we've finished this job. What's the suggestion?"

"Wait for a week. I'll watch what happens tomorrow, and be able to make sure we don't make any wrong moves. I'll get to know the place—might see some snags that don't show up yet. How about it? I can lend you twenty if it would help."

"We'll wait," said Steve.

He stepped out of the call-box, looked along the narrow street, and saw Alec step out of the corner shop – he had telephoned from there. He didn't look round. Steve stood still a few minutes, before turning into the pub. He had a week on hand which he hadn't planned, but he told himself that young Alec had a wise head on his shoulders, while he himself had nearly made the fatal mistake of acting on impulse again. He always wanted things done yesterday.

He grinned as he stared across the saloon bar, where Joyce was drawing dark ale. She glanced up, caught his eyes, and gave the quick, pleased smile which she reserved for him. He strode across. No one else was waiting to be served.

"What's yours?" she asked.

"Whisky-and-soda," said Steve. "I want to get my strength up."

She laughed, poured the drink, pushed a syphon of soda towards him, and then produced a copy of the *Daily Mirror* from the shelf beneath the bar. It was folded to the composite pictures, and so that when he glanced down at them, he saw them.

The glass was half way to his lips. He held it there poised for a moment, and an icy spasm went up and down his spine. Then he put the glass to his lips and tossed his head back.

"That one on the right," Joyce said. "Isn't it like Alec Gool?"

Chapter Sixteen

Big Snatch

"I can see what you mean," Steve said carefully, "but I shouldn't have recognised the likeness myself."

He sat at the kitchen table, leaning back a little on his chair, outwardly quite calm. Joyce was pouring coffee. It was surprising how easily and naturally they lived together – at moments like these, there was a cosy intimacy which in some ways was better even than being in bed together. He had come on ahead, and had been waiting for her. She pushed the brown sugar towards him.

"But it is like him, Steve, isn't it?"

"In a way, I suppose it is."

"You don't think it's him?"

"From what I know of Alec Gool he wouldn't have the guts to take part in a wages snatch or to rob a blind man," said Steve. "He likes life easy. Too easy." He put a small spoonful of sugar into the cup, stirred, then sipped his coffee. "What about the other one? Got anybody in line for him?"

"No," said Joyce. She glanced down at the newspaper, but not very intently; she had looked at it so much in the past two days that she could almost shut her eyes and picture it. "No, I can't say I have. Have you?"

"I knew a chap named Bennett who was like him – we were on a ship on the East African run. Now he would have cut his own mother's throat for a five pound note." Steve laughed, and sipped more coffee. "Talked to anyone else about this, Joycey?"

"No," she replied, quite matter-of-fact. "I wouldn't like to start a rumour even about Alec Gool. You know how fast they spread. But if you'd agreed with me—"

"I tell you, I can just about see what you mean."

"Well, if you agreed with me altogether, it would be different."

He looked at her over the rim of his cup.

"How would it be different?"

"Well, we'd have to do something about it, wouldn't we?"

"Would we?"

"Well, if he killed a man—"

"Joyce," Steve said, "don't turn stool-pigeon for anyone. That's one thing I couldn't take. Understand? What Alec Gool or anyone else does is no business of ours unless we get mixed up in it—and I don't intend to. I've seen too much happen when people start squealing. I've seen pretty women like you who telephoned the cops, being rushed to hospital a few days later, their cheeks cut open—or their eyes closed for the rest of their lives with vitriol."

"Steve! Don't!"

"I don't want anything to happen to your face, I like it too much." Steve leaned across the table, took her face in his hands, drew her forward, made her purse her lips and kissed her lightly. "It's a very nice face," he said, "and you've got beautiful eyes. Didn't I tell you?"

She managed to say through her pouting lips – lips kept in that shape by his hands:

"I believe you did happen to mention it, once upon a time. It was a long while ago, though."

"And it will be a long while before I tell you again," said Steve. "Make the best of it." He let her go. "Heard anyone at the pub talk about young Alec?"

"Oh, they say he's a queer."

"By queer, you mean a homosexual," said Steve. He wrinkled up his nose. "Don't worry about calling a spade a spade or a homo a homo, Joycey. You due for a holiday?" The question came out so unexpectedly that for a moment Joyce could only sit and stare.

"Well, I am really, but—"

"Take it, right away," ordered Steve.

"But Mr Harris—"

"Never mind Harris. You're the best bar-maid in London, and he ought to know it. I'm going to sign on again next week. Money's running low. I won't be away for long—a couple of months, maybe—and I'd like to have a honeymoon before I leave."

"Honeymoon!" Joyce cried.

She saw on the instant that he hadn't meant that literally, and she was too suddenly and acutely disappointed to pretend that it didn't matter. After her cry, the end of the word seemed to echo about the kitchen. "Honey—*moooooon!*" She had raised her hands in the momentary excitement, and they were still in front of her. Very slowly, she lowered them; as slowly, she shifted back in her chair. All the time, Steve stared at her, his eyes expressionless, all the humour, all the drollness gone.

At last, Joyce looked away.

"I'll get some more coffee," she said, and pushed her chair back.

"Joyce—"

"It's all right," she said, getting up and stepping to the gas-stove. "I should have known you weren't a marrying man. It's all right." Her hand was only a little unsteady as she poured coffee into her cup. She turned round. "More for you?"

Steve stood up, took her cup away, then dropped his hand to her wrist.

"Joycey—"

Now she looked him straight in the eye.

"It's all right, I tell you. I should have known better. You don't owe me anything—you've never made me any promises. I can't help it if I love you so much, but—I'm not a fool. How long have you to go away for, do you say?"

He didn't answer, but held her wrist.

"I tell you it's all right. *Steve!*" She tried to free herself, but the grip of his fingers was like steel. Slowly, he drew her towards him, and she could not resist his physical strength; after a moment she did not try.

"There's something I want to tell you," he said. "I'm not the marrying kind—I've never been married and I never expected that I would want to be. You're the first woman I've ever met who even made me think about it. But I'm not right for you, Joyce. Not as a husband. I'm no good to anyone as a husband. I live my life the way I've got to, and it doesn't have any room for a—*good* woman."

She didn't speak.

"What I meant is that we could do with a few days holiday out of London. It would be almost the same thing as a honeymoon. I thought we might go to Brighton, or Bournemouth. Like a few days holiday, with me?"

"I'm not sure I can get the time off."

"Just walk out on Harris. He'll take you back with open arms."

"It's no use, I'm not sure," Joyce said. "Let me think about it, Steve. Do you want more coffee, or don't you?"

After a long pause, still holding her, he said: "So it's like that. Okay, sweetie, you think about it. I'll leave you to sleep on it, in fact. Only don't forget this—say yes, say no, it won't make any difference to the way I feel about you. I've never met a woman I liked more or respected more, and if I never had another woman in my life I'd be satisfied." For the first time since that cry of *"Honeymoon!"* his eyes took on a spark of humour. "In bed or out of bed, you're the tops for me. I'll be seeing you. Be ready with your answer any time after nine o'clock in the morning."

Her heart and the coldness which he had put into it, were already melting.

"Steve—"

"'Night, sweetie," he said, and gave her a hug and a squeeze and a kiss on the forehead. He grabbed his coat from the back of his chair, and fumbled it, as if he was upset, too. He put it on, and went out. He moved with such speed that he was closing the street door before she reached the end of the passage from the kitchen. She hurried into the bedroom, in time to see him walking past the window, but did not know whether he glanced at the window or not. She stood for a long time, pale light from a street lamp softening her features, gleaming upon the tears in her eyes. Her heart beat very fast; there was a kind of ecstasy that was also pain.

At last, she went back to the kitchen.

"If you're not careful you'll lose him altogether," she said. She picked up a coffee cup, and noticed the *Daily Mirror* and the drawing of "Alec Gool" again. There was something about the way the light fell on the drawings which made them look different, and the second man, the man whose face was only half-finished, seemed to come more alive. As she stared, an awful flash of suspicion entered her head. Was that *Steve?*

She snatched the paper up. The likeness – the swift, passing likeness to Steve faded.

She moved to go to the stove and the sink – and kicked something which slithered along the oilcloth. It was small and dark – a book of some kind. She bent down and picked it up, and saw the coat of arms on the front, the name Joseph Bennett on a white inset at the top, a number below. In gilt lettering there were the words *British Passport*. She thought vaguely, idly, that it was strange Steve should have another man's passport in his pocket. She opened it – and Steve's face was there in front of her. It wasn't really a good photograph but was unquestionably of him.

"Steve," she said, in a puzzled voice. "What's on?"

She looked at the page opposite the photograph, and glanced down, saw the signature *Jos. Bennett*. She was so intent and so bewildered that she didn't hear the slight sound at the door. She did not hear the very soft footfall. She stared down.

"Steve," she repeated.

"Want me?" Steve asked.

She jumped wildly, and swung round, the passport still in her hand. He stood in the doorway, the top of his head touching the lintel. She had never seen his face so set, so stern, so severe. He did not move, yet he gave her the impression that he was going to pounce on her.

"I dropped something out of my pocket," he said. "My passport." At last he moved. He did not look away from her, and she experienced a shivery kind of fear, but didn't shrink, just held it out to him.

"I wish you hadn't looked at it," he said.

"So—so do I."

"Didn't know my real name was Bennett, did you?"

"Your—*real* name."

"That's right." He opened the passport and ran a finger down the descriptive column opposite the photograph. "I use Steve Stevens for convenience sometimes—and it sticks. I was introduced to you as Steve Stevens, and there wasn't any point in explaining. I didn't know I was going to fall in love with you, did I?"

"Steve, that—that's your *real* name?"

"It is."

"Oh," she said. "I thought—I thought you had a forged passport. I thought you were going to run away from something."

"The trouble with you is you get too many ideas," he said, half jesting, half roughly. "You think too much. I'm going on a trip to get more money in my belt so that I can waste it on you." He tucked the passport into his pocket.

"I've changed my mind, I'm staying the night," he went on, and the gleam lit up his eyes again. "And whether you like it or not, sweetie, you're coming for a holiday with me to Brighton or Bournemouth – take your choice. I'm not letting you out of my sight until I step on board my ship." He stretched out his arms and took hers and drew her to him, and crushed her close.

She lay sleeping.

He lay thinking: how am I going to work this out? Why did she have to see that bloody thing?

And he thought: she could help me to hang.

Roger went to bed at about the same time as Joyce and Steve Stevens, and for once dropped off to sleep almost immediately. He woke before any of the rest of the household, a few minutes before seven. He was wide awake almost at once, and by the time he was downstairs, making tea, had already decided what he would do during the day. Before he left, soon after eight o'clock and while the boys were still dreamy, Janet said: "You look much better, darling—Bennison meant a lot to you, didn't he?"

"Too much," said Roger, briskly. "I was too worked up over avenging him, but I won't make that mistake again." He gave her a hug which made her gasp, kissed her lightly on the nose and the forehead, so that he should not show too much of his feeling, and went off.

At half past eight, he was in the office. By the time Cope arrived at ten to nine, he had pencilled out his plans.

"We'll send a man to each of these firms" – he gave Cope the list of places where Charley Blake had worked – "with the composite picture, and try to find out if anyone answering the description worked with Blake. If there's a bite of any kind, I'll go out and talk to the people myself. All clear?"

"As mud," said Cope, sniffing. "You've got a hope, you have. But I daresay it's worth trying. Who'd you like me to send?"

"Who's in?"

"I'll find out," said Cope. "That reminds me, did you hear about the big job last night? Looks like a cert for you. Gang blasted a way to the vaults of the *Midpro* in Watford. Got away with ninety thousand quid, mostly in marked notes. One bank guard's okay, they just knocked him out. The other might die."

"Oh," said Roger, and felt the sense of shock which news of big jobs of this kind always created. Cope was right: this job would almost certainly fall into his lap. "Jack," he said, "I'm going out to see these factories myself."

Cope grinned.

"Thought you might," he said. "But don't forget that if you handle the Watford job you'll get your picture in the paper again. They like our glamour boy."

"I'll be seeing you," Roger said.

He had a sense of guilt mingling with a sense of satisfaction as he drove away from the Yard. The guilt soon faded. Any one of half-a-dozen – perhaps a dozen – men could tackle the new investigation as well as he could, but no one else had the same complete grasp of the Covent Garden affair.

He drove to the market first, had a word with Revel & Son – and found that the manager, Kent, was back at his desk. Roger had not known Kent well, and was surprised to find him so old, and with a constant tremor in his right hand; that might be the result of shock. He asked more questions about Charley Blake, to refresh his memory, left the offices, and went into the market itself.

Calwin was loading up with baskets full of Beauty of Bath, the earliest crop of English apples. Two men were helping him. Roger counted seven baskets and wondered how many he would take. He stopped at nine.

"So you've come again," he said, squinting down at Roger. "Thought you'd forgotten me. I've got to get this lot over to a van the other side of the market—if you want to talk you'll have to trot alongside me like a good boy."

Roger grinned.

"I'll pick up the apples you drop."

"Me *drop* a basket? Haven't done that since I first learned me job." Calwin strode out, deliberately taking long strides, as if he wanted to make it difficult for Roger to keep up. Other porters, trucks, boxes of fruit on the pavement, men talking and haggling about prices – all of these things made straight-forward conversation difficult.

"Dunno that I can tell you anything else," Calwin said. *"Mind that lemon.* Don't know what they pay you for. I solved *half* the case for you – got a letter thanking me from a cove who signed hisself Deputy Commander. You put him up to that? *Mind that rotten cabbage.* If you did, you forgot to tell him to put in the reward." Calwin grinned broadly all the time; he looked more than ever like Cope, with his wobbly Adam's apple and his half closed eyes. "As a matter of fact I was going to tell you. I've been thinking. *Don't knock those avocado pears over, they're the dearest fruit in the market.* Keep looking at that picture, too—the one of the killer. Keep doing what you told me, Gawd knows why, and going back to the place where I was when it happened and trying to remember anything that I'd forgotten before. Interesting—you'd be surprised. Do you know I can remember seeing seven more people, when I come to think hard about it, than I did at the time. How about that? First time, I told you I just knew there were people. Now I can tell you the colour of their hair. Funny thing, the mind. *Keep your hands off them peaches.* There's one thing I remembered which might 'elp you, but then again it might not. 'Arf a mo'."

He stopped at an open lorry which was heavily laden. A porter called out to him, cheerfully. Two men came from one of the shops, as Calwin did that curious acrobatic body twist, and lowered the baskets.

"There you are, not a scratch on 'em. Sign here." He pulled a small book from his paper pocket, with some carbon paper between the sheets. "Nine boxes filled to the brim—ta." A man scribbled a signature, Calwin tore off one sheet and handed it to him, and grinned. "Can't stop, I got to see a man about a cop." He rested a big calloused hand in comradely fashion on Roger's shoulder. "Betcher couldn't guess what I've remembered."

"You win your bet," said Roger, trying to conceal his impatience.

"Notice you never put no money on it. Are all coppers mean? All right, Handsome, I won't keep you in suspense no longer. The cove what used the knife had had plenty of practice, you know that. But he had something else—a look of *surprise*. Get me?"

Roger said, softly: "A startled look? As if he'd seen something he hadn't expected?"

"Or someone," Calwin breathed. "Now tell me you'd already guessed that."

Roger didn't tell him so; but he felt more hopeful than he had before, as if this were a good omen.

"One of these days I'll buy you a dinner," he said.

"Never mind buying me a dinner, my wife feeds me all right," said Calwin. There was a different, almost anxious note in his voice. "Tell you what I would like—me and me kids. Got three, all boys. I'd like to have a dekko at the Yard. Kind of Crooks' Tour, see." He did not laugh at his own joke. "Think you can fix it?"

"I can and I will," said Roger at once. "You can call it a date."

Calwin's eyes lit up.

"How about Monday week?" he said. "The kids have got a half-day, and I can take one off. Okay?"

"Monday week it is. Two-thirty at the Yard, and if it's at all possible I'll take you round myself," promised Roger. "Thanks for the latest clue." He put his hand to his forehead and hurried off.

As he got to the wheel of his car he felt another surge of excitement and optimism.

Sitting on the verandah of the hotel room overlooking the sea and the piers, Steve Stevens *alias* Joseph Bennett trimmed his nails. Joyce, stretched out on a low chair with only a flimsy pair of panties on, and loving the sun, reached across and took the scissors from him.

"I'll do that right thumb," she said.

"Okay," said Steve, and grinned and stared at her legs. "And then I'll give you a nice rub all over with sun-tan oil. How's that for a treat?"

Chapter Seventeen

No – No – Yes

Roger came down the steps of the big Hoover Factory, after a futile half-hour. Everyone had been eager to help, and several people remembered Charley Blake, who had left because the journey from his Fulham home was too long, but no one remembered anyone who might fit in with the description of a tall lean man who was also a friend of Charley, or else knew him well.

The same story came from Wimpey's, except that Charley Blake had left the job at Wembley because the firm had wanted a younger man.

It was half-past twelve when Roger reached Linstone's, who had a sprawling two-storey building on the Great West Road, not far from the Gillette Tower. It was painted white. He noticed an armoured van at the side of the building, and two men came up to him as he approached the gate.

"Mind waiting for a few minutes, sir?" one asked.

"Why?" inquired Roger.

"Security reasons, sir."

"Glad to see some precautions being taken," said Roger. "Wages money?"

"Hardly any business of yours, sir, is it?" The big, burly man now standing just outside the car was respectful but firm.

Roger chuckled.

"You'd be surprised," he said, and lit a cigarette.

He saw the armoured car, which was facing the Great West Road, and backed on to a little loading bay. On the right of the bay was a white building marked: *Trade Stores*. On the left were offices which were not marked. As far as he could see, the loading bay was in a recess, and anything wanted for or from the *Trade Stores* went into or came from it. Presumably the wages office was approached from the door on the other side of the bay.

He did not give that any thought, except the normal ones – what kind of a security risk was it? With as many guards about as this, he didn't think there would be much. He counted two at the gates – the man who had made him stop, and another – and there were at least four inside up by the armoured van.

At last, it moved off.

"Mind if I have your name now, sir?" this guard said.

"West," said Roger and handed over a card. For a moment it was held in thick, flat-topped fingers – and then the half-expected explosion came.

"Superintendent West?"

Roger put his head closer to the open window, and looked up.

"Think your warehouse people could spare me a few minutes? And your chief security officer?"

"I *am* the chief security officer, sir—name of Soames. Can't understand why I didn't recognise you, I really can't. My office is just round behind the gate house. Like to drive round, sir – I'll meet you there."

Roger noticed that Soames was watching the armoured van. The other security men dispersed, and cars began to move, so there was a restriction of movement during the actual unloading of the money. Soames was pretty thorough.

Soames was in his small office.

"I wasn't at the Yard or the Divisions, sir – Transport Police, that was my job before I came here. All the same, I should have recognised you." That failure obviously worried him. "Now if there's anything I can do to help—"

Roger explained.

"I remember Charley Blake very well," said Soames. "One of the nicest chaps you'd ever come across. Spent most of his life at sea. I'm trying to think why he left. Something to do with where he lived – kept trying to get a job nearer his home, I think. I know there was no trouble." He studied the composite picture. "You know, it does remind me of someone," he said. "I can't say who, at the moment. Charley was in the stores part of the time, I remember— warehouseman most of the time in fact, gave us a hand with security on special occasions, like today. There *was* one tall lean man … but let's go into the warehouse, shall we?"

They went inside, from the loading bay. The Trade Stores warehouse was very large, but on one floor only. It was a honeycomb of passages and bins of green steel – rather like a vast set of pigeon-holes. These were one side of a long counter which stretched from the loading bay door to another door nearer the gatehouse.

All the bins were stacked with motor car accessories. Several men were at the bins, and two at the counter serving three men on the counters near the door. Anyone who came to collect goods stood at this counter, with his back to the windows. The lighting was excellent – everything about the place seemed to be well-organised.

Roger noticed a youngish man with beautifully-groomed hair disappearing into one of the bins, but took no special notice.

"Will," Soames called, and an elderly man with a fringe of grey hair and a large bald spot turned round. "I want you to meet Superintendent West, of the Yard."

"Very pleased to meet you, sir."

"This is the Trade Stores Manager, Mr Forsyte," said Soames. "Will, Mr West wants to know …"

He explained as precisely and as lucidly as Roger had to him. The old man kept nodding – in understanding rather than recognition, Roger thought, and for the first time he felt almost despondent.

"Yes, there was a man answering that description," said the manager, quite matter-of-factly. "A man named Stevens. He was here in the Trade Warehouse for a few weeks as a packer. I understood that he was a seaman but liked to spend some of the winter on land. He and Charley knew each other quite well. They'd been to sea together, and had a lot in common. As a matter of fact, I think it was Charley who introduced him to us."

Roger's heart suddenly began to race.

"What kind of chap was he?"

"Bit sarcastic, as a matter of fact—could be funny in a way, but he could be pretty nasty, too. I had to get rid of him because he got too fresh with some of the girls. Some of them fell for him, but he wasn't interested in push-overs. He started some nonsense with the wife of one of the charge-hands. The only thing I could do was put him out—so he went out."

"He resent it?"

"Didn't seem to, particularly," said Forsyte. He looked down at the composite drawing again, and frowned. "It is and it isn't like him, if you see what I mean." Roger didn't, yet. The manager led the way into his small, tidy office, and took the picture to a window. He studied it from several perspectives, his head going to and fro like a sparrow's. Suddenly he said in a tone nearer excitement: "Now that's more like him. See? That shadow from the window is falling across it, it's broken the outline a bit—here, wait a minute! I believe I've got a photograph of him."

He rummaged in the centre drawer of his desk, and brought out a photograph of a big van, made up for some advertising stunt for Linstone Tyres. There were some bathing beauties on it, and several men – and in one corner was a man standing looking on.

"That's him," said Forsyte. "It's not very good, mind you, but you might be able to get it blown up. We didn't use this picture, and I don't think he was in any of those we used for the publicity. I can easily check."

"Will you?" asked Roger.

"How about having some lunch with me while Mr Forsyte's making sure?" suggested Soames.

At three o'clock, Roger left the factory with the print carefully flattened in his brief-case. Stevens had not appeared in any of the other pictures, but under a magnifying glass this likeness showed up well.

He was at the Yard in half an hour, and went straight up to *Photography.*

"How soon can you rush me an enlargement?" he asked the man in charge.

"Give me a couple of hours?"

"Right," said Roger. "Don't be any longer." He hurried down to his office, and telephoned Revel & Son, spoke to Kent and asked him to have someone send a message to Calwin the porter. Would Calwin either wait at the market or be at the Yard by half past five?

"I'll talk to him myself," said Kent. "I'll call you back, Mr West." He rang off, his quavering voice still choking in Roger's ears. He was back in ten minutes. "He will come to you, Mr West—he has promised to be at Scotland Yard by half past five exactly."

For the occasion, Calwin had had a hair cut and a shave. He also wore a white collar and check blue and white tie instead of a choker. He was exactly die same in his laconic, mock-truculent manner, but when he saw the enlargement of Stevens's photograph, his eyes seemed to blaze.

"That's the man all right. That's the killer! I'd stake my bottom dollar on it."

Joyce Conway had seldom felt happier than she did that night, the second at Brighton.

In a way, the clash with Steve had brought things to a head and cleared the air. She knew how things were now, and acknowledged the fact that Steve would never marry her; she would have to put up with the situation as it was. The fear that he might be going away for good had died, and the suspicion roused by the name of Bennett on the passport had faded, too. He was going away for a few weeks, that was all. And he had said that he loved her.

She sensed that it had been a difficult thing for him to avow, and she sensed that it had been true, too. They had thoroughly enjoyed the two days at Brighton so far – and in her commonsense way, she told herself that this was because she was being grateful for what she had, and wasn't wishing for something out of reach.

The hotel, one of the best on Brighton front, was an old-fashioned one. Steve had taken the best room available, with that terrace overlooking the sea, and at night the swish and sizzle of the water through the pebbles on the beach kept her pleasantly and drowsily awake just long enough for her to appreciate the fact that Steve was lying beside her in the big double bed.

He didn't snore, that was one thing! In those days so long ago, Tom had snored.

They had been to *Ice Follies,* at the Rink, and were strolling home, arm-in-arm, with the stars and a half moon shining on the calm sea. London, distant lands, doubts and suspicions and fears were all forgotten. Lights blazed from the hotel. Cars were parked outside it, and a few men and girls stood about.

She noticed a man on his own, and heard a hissing sound, as if someone was trying to attract their attention. She looked round. For a moment she thought that Steve was edgy – his arm seemed to stiffen – and then he relaxed.

"You go up to the room," he said, when they were in the hotel. "I want to find out about the coach trips tomorrow. When I get upstairs I shall expect to see you in that shameful new negligee—"

"Don't say things like that so *loud,* Steve!"

He laughed, and saw her to the lift; in little courtesies he treated her as a real lady, and she had neither suspicion nor premonition of trouble as she went into the room. A maid had turned down the bedclothes, and the new black negligee, bought only that afternoon, was on it, looking beautiful.

Joyce's eyes glowed.

Downstairs, outside among the cars and in the shadows, Steve said to Alec Gool: "What the hell are you doing here, you bloody young pup?"

"Take it easy, Steve," Alec protested. "You've got a shock coming to you, and you had to know quick." Before Steve could comment, he went on: "Unless you'd rather get it from the busies."

"Keep your voice down!"

"Getting nervous?" Alec said, but behind the jeering in his voice there was a sense of urgency. "Let's take a walk."

They walked down to the beach, where only the couples were now, many lying close together in the shelters, some in the shelter of the boats drawn up away from the sea.

"Steve," Alec said, "that copper West was at Linstone's this afternoon, asking about anyone who knew Charley Blake. You knew Charley Blake. I often wondered why you put that knife in his guts."

Steve didn't speak; his feet crunched the pebbles.

"I tried to get everything out of the manager, but he's an old flicker. Wouldn't come across at all. But West was around for a couple of hours or more. And I heard the manager mention you."

Steve caught his breath.

"Sure about that?"

"I'm sure."

After a pause, Steve said softly: "It's time you knocked that grin off your face. If we'd done that job this morning, when I wanted to, we could have been away by now." He felt the soft breeze off the sea on his face. Haze misted the lights at the ends of the piers and at the hotel when he glanced up towards it. "So they got round to naming me as a pal of Charley Blake."

"I told you so. I often wondered—"

"Well, you can stop wondering," Steve said. There was a shocked edge to his voice. "The moment I saw Charley I knew he recognised me. If I hadn't put him away we wouldn't have had a chance. It was too late to back out after they started on Bennison." He wiped his forehead. "That means they'll get on to me."

"That's right," Alec said. "You won't be able to fool around with li'l old Joycey any longer. Your—"

"If you talk about Joyce I'll break your neck."

"Eh, eh, eh!" protested Alec, backing away. "Serious as that, eh? All right, forget it – I didn't mean any offence. The truth remains—you've got to hide somewhere."

"I know it."

"I know a place," said Alec.

"Where?"

"There's an Australian ship in at Matt's Dock—came in last night. The skipper's okay—it's the ship I think we could get out on, next

Friday. The skipper would let you sign on for the trip now. If you get there by night, no one will see you on board. How about it?"

"I don't want to panic," Steve said.

"Who's talking about panic?" demanded Alec. "I saw the way they handled the dough at Linstone's, and you're dead right. With tear-gas, handled the way you said, it's a cinch. You could come off the *Fernando* next Thursday morning, pinch a van and drive straight from there to the factory. It wouldn't be any problem. You'd get past the gateguards without any trouble—they wouldn't be looking for anyone *coming away* from a ship. Then I could take the van in later and we could get aboard after dark. How about it?"

Steve said, slowly: "I'll say one thing for you, you've got guts. Some of the security men might recognise me but I can fool 'em with a moustache and cheek pads. They won't see me for long."

"It's our big chance, Steve."

"Sure. This Aussie skipper—"

"I can fix him."

"Okay," said Steve. "I'll go and get my things and make some excuse to Joyce. Then—"

He broke off. In the dim light, Alec was staring at him, and there was a subtle change in the youth's manner. He stood with his eyes narrowed, and in a curiously aggressive attitude as he said:

"No dice, Steve."

"No dice, what?"

"You can't see Joyce any more."

"Don't be a bloody fool! All my clothes—"

"I wouldn't trust you with her for five minutes," Alec said. His voice was very soft and there was a note of menace in it, perhaps also a note of fear. "You're gone on her, and you'd let something out. It's bye-bye, Joyce. You won't need all those slap-up clothes, anyhow. I've got a car waiting, Steve."

They stood motionless for a long time. Steve Stevens was thinking about Joyce – and much, much more. There was the danger, the incredible fact that the police had got on to Linstone's, that he had led them to the factory by killing Charley Blake. So there would be a search for him under the name of Stevens – which meant that the police would know where to look for him tomorrow. They would talk to a dozen people who could name him.

He knew their methods only too well. They weren't brilliant, but they got their man – and unless he was very careful, they would get him. Alec was right; the cunning young slob was smart, and he had never been smarter than about this. The sensible thing to do was go away with him.

He could telephone Joyce. By tomorrow the police would question her, so she would know the truth about him, she would soon get used to it. If things had been different he might have married her, but now – he had to face cold, brutal facts.

Alec was right – except for one thing: he didn't know that Joyce knew the name on the passport.

Chapter Eighteen

Decision

Not far away from the spot where the two men stood, a girl sat up, and said: "Look what you've done to my bra." A man murmured something lazily, and the girl giggled. On the beach itself, a six-some of teenagers walked with their hands linked, their footsteps strange and almost eerie in the shingle. Here, the silence between Alec and Steve was so great that Steve's breathing was audible.

"You don't have any time to think," said Alec. "This is a must."

"Shut up," Steve said.

"I tell you—"

Steve shot out his right hand and clutched the youth's neck so tightly that Alec gave a choking gasp, and his body sagged. Steve didn't let go. In that moment rage took hold of him and was almost ungovernable; he could have squeezed and squeezed until the life died out of the youth. Alec clutched at his wrist, then kicked at his knees and caught him on the shin.

Steve let him go.

"You must be crazy," Alec muttered hoarsely.

"No one tells me what I've got to do," said Steve. "I'm going to see Joyce. I've got something to say to her. She's reliable."

"Reliable? She'll squeal as soon as—"

"I told you to shut up," Steve said. "I meant it. I'll be back in half an hour. Where's the car?"

"Listen, if you tell her where you're going—"

"I won't tell her a thing she doesn't know," Steve said. He turned away. "Where's the car?"

"It's—outside the hotel."

"Be there in half an hour," ordered Steve.

He walked ahead, stumbling over shingle, striding up the ramp, then on the promenade. He looked across at the hotel. There was a light on in his room, of course, but the blind was drawn, and he could see very little, although there was shadowy movement against the blind.

He didn't go straight across the road, but strode along the promenade, trying to think clearly. That passport *mattered*. Once he was across the Channel, he would need it. Wherever he went, he would need it. He had to slip out of the skin of Steve Stevens into that of Joseph Bennett – the transition was his whole future. With that passport and that certificate he could get anywhere, but if the police knew the *alias,* then every port, every ship, all the customs authorities would be alerted. He had no doubts about the thoroughness of the police once they were after a murderer.

His whole future depended on that new identity – and Joyce knew about it.

He was sweating.

If he walked out on her now, she would tell the police. If he told her the truth, sooner or later she would tell them – being what she was, it would eat into her conscience, unless – unless they were together.

If they got married –

That wouldn't do. The police would not be able to make her give evidence against him, but that wasn't what he needed to prevent. It was that fateful piece of knowledge that mattered: the *alias.*

He ought to make sure she could never tell the police; he ought to kill her.

He was still walking. Up here, near Hove and the residential part of the district, fewer people were about. He noticed few of them, although he did see two policemen walking along together. One was whistling faintly. Steve took no notice of them, reached a place where the promenade was under repair and a deviation was necessary, and stopped. This was as far as he should go. He stared out to sea – his sanctuary.

Yes, he ought to kill her. He had three murders in his past, one more should make no difference.

Kill her?

How did he know that she would go to the police? She loved him, didn't she? He felt differently towards her than he had to any woman in the past, and if she loved him, would she betray him? He was listening to the insidious voice of Alec too much; what did the kid know about older people, about mature men and women?

He swung round and started back, and as the lights of the hotel drew nearer, his stride lengthened. He could see the light at that corner window; Joyce would be wondering what had happened to him.

The disquiet which was never far away was back with Joyce, seeming worse because she had been so happy during the evening; and she believed that Steve had been, too. She kept remembering that hissing sound – had someone been attracting his attention? Once her thoughts started wandering, all the old half formed suspicions came back. Alec Gool's likeness to that picture, the fleeting likeness of Steve to the other, the *alias,* his attitude. There was so much crowding her mind and she did not want to think about any of it, but every moment that Steve was away brought more urgently worrying thoughts.

The floor creaked, outside the door – it always did.

Was this Steve?

The handle rattled, and then turned.

She slid out of bed quickly, knowing he would want to see her standing in her negligee. It was soft, clinging, lovely, voluptuous. She caught a glimpse of herself in the mirror; it was almost transparent.

Steve came in. She expected his eyes to light up the moment he saw her. She expected him to stop with his fingers on the door, eyeing her up and down in that bold, wicked, wonderful way of his.

He closed the door, looking into her eyes; his gaze didn't drop.

"Joyce," he said, "we've got to get out of here."

She drew in a deep breath.

"Get dressed, quick," he said.

She could hardly believe it – but almost at once the fears which she had known when at home came crowding back.

"Steve—"

"Don't argue! Get dressed quick." He strode towards the bathroom door, stopping in front of the case which was open on a stool just by it.

"Listen, Steve."

He swung round on her, his eyes blazing.

"Do what you're told!"

In all her life, she had never been talked to like that; *never*. She had never known a man look as Steve looked now, either; as if he hated. But fear was cut away, anger blazed up in her – born of shock, of disappointment, of the fear. Instead of moving to her clothes on a chair, she raised her hands in front of her breasts and said sharply:

"I won't do any such thing! And I won't be spoken to like that."

He said: "Why, you—" and suddenly moved towards her, his hands outstretched, fingers crooked as if he would curl them round her neck. She was so shocked that she couldn't even back away.

"Steve!"

He actually touched her neck with his hands, and his cold fingers sent a shiver through her body. She struck at his arms, and dodged back, banged her thigh against a corner of the dressing-table, and gasped with pain. At least she freed herself.

"*Steve*," she whispered. "What's got into you?"

He stood with his hands outstretched but some of the tension gone from his body. The glitter had faded from his eyes, too. He licked his lips. She could not tell how beautiful the terror had made her, and still made her.

He said in a grating whisper, as if the words were being forced out of him:

"I'm in trouble. The police might be here soon—certainly by the morning. I've got to get out of the country." He made himself look at her. "I *ought* to kill you." There, it was out. "Because you know about that passport. But I can't. I can't. Joyce—we're going away. I know a place we can hide out until it's blown over. Then we'll get out of the country. You and me. We can get married. We can live together." He was pausing between each word, now, as if the power which had driven him to say this was gradually dying. "Joyce—we've got to get away."

She could ask him why: she could want to know what crime he had committed. She stood there, hands crossed in front of breast, white body showing so vividly through the black negligee. If she did ask – God knew how much longer he could stand it. *He ought to kill her.*

She said: "All right, Steve. I'll be ready in ten minutes." No questions, no arguments, just quick and ready acquiescence; of course he could rely on her!

"I don't know whether the skipper of the *Fernando* will take a woman on board," Alec muttered.

"He'll take this woman," Steve said. "You concentrate on your driving."

He sat next to Alec as the little Ford hummed towards London. Joyce sat in the back, her eyes closed except at odd moments when she looked at the back of his head.

She had committed herself now; her life was his.

The photograph of Steve Stevens was distributed to all London and Home Counties police stations that night and early the next morning, as well as to all ports, airports and railway terminals. The message with it ran: *Wanted for the murder of a wages guard. Known to be dangerous. Believed to work with a slim, well-dressed youth, who is also dangerous.*

Roger studied the photograph and the caption when he reached the Yard, just before half past eight next morning. He felt on top of the world, as if it could not be long before the arrest was made.

At nine o'clock, the first report came in from the East End Division.

"We know this chap," Golloway said. "Sure he's as dangerous as you make out, Handsome?"

"Yes."

"I'll do a bit of quiet checking," said Golloway. "I'll let you know."

Reports began to come in one after the other, from the Thames Division, from other Divisions in the East End of London, from the City Police, and divisional sub-stations. By half past ten, two shipping agencies, three shipping lines and one shipping employment agency were on the line to report that they knew Stevens. Swiftly, a dossier was built up about the missing man; half-hour by half-hour Roger waited for news that he had been found.

At half past eleven, Golloway was on the line again.

"No luck, yet, Handsome. He's not at his lodgings."

"Sure about that?"

"Positive—I've been to the place myself. I was careful, but it seemed pretty sure. I'm covering everything. If I get a line, I'll be in touch."

"He couldn't have been tipped off, could he?" asked Cope, gloomily. "I've seen him before somewhere myself, too—can't place him though. Think it's worth looking through the Rogues' Gallery for him?"

"No," said Roger, and abruptly changed his mind. It would give him something to do. He spent an hour scrutinising photographs of men roughly similar to Stevens in appearance, and then there was a call for him.

"It's Golloway again," said the East End superintendent. "Still haven't got him—and there's a funny bit of news." "What is it?"

"He's been going around with a woman named Conway, a barmaid at the Hornpipe, here in my manor. Nice enough woman, widow, good reputation, until she took up with Stevens. He's been spending a lot of time at her place, but she left with him three days ago. She said she was going to Brighton—told the milkman she was, anyhow."

"Keep at it. I'll contact Brighton," Roger said. He went downstairs, to find Cope writing busily.

"Got something, Handsome," he volunteered. "Stevens was at the Old Mast Hotel, Brighton, until late last night. Been staying there two or three days, with a woman. They cleared out during the night. No one knows where they went. Not much doubt Stevens was tipped off, is there?"

"Looks like it," agreed Roger, concealing his disappointment. "The docks ought to be combed, and we want a list of all ships which are due to sail anytime this week. I think I'll go over to the docks myself."

"Hope it's not a waste of time," said Cope, gloomily.

As the day went by, with dozens of reports that Stevens had been seen in the past few weeks, the hopes of a quick arrest faded. No reports came of the association of Stevens with any youth who answered the description of the driver of the Covent Garden van, but there were stories that Stevens had been seen with Marriott and Dorris several times. That association was gradually pieced together, dossiers grew and grew, until they knew practically all there was to know about Stevens, and the woman, Conway. There were odd rumours that a youth named Gool had been seen with Stevens occasionally, but according to one or two witnesses, Gool had signed on as a deck-hand on a cargo vessel which had left for the Far East a week ago. Certainly he had told his landlady he was going, and had left a case of clothes in her keeping.

On the Tuesday, every newspaper in the country carried pictures of Stevens and Joyce Conway.

On the Thursday, even Roger was beginning to believe that they had managed to get out of the country, like Gool.

On that Thursday morning, Steve said to Joyce: "I've got to go out today, sweetie—got something to attend to. I'll be back by two o'clock, and we'll be off on the afternoon tide. As soon as we're at sea you can go up on deck by day as well as by night. Okay?"

"I'm all right, Steve," Joyce said in a subdued voice. "I don't care what happens so long as we're together. You—you will come back, won't you?"

"I'll come back," Steve assured her.

He went off in a van which he said Alec Gool had fixed, and Joyce watched him through the porthole of the cabin she snared with him.

She wondered if he was going to do a "job".

She could not desert him, could not betray him, but day by day she wondered whether it was true that she didn't care what happened provided they were together.

Chapter Nineteen

Big Raid

At Linstone's, the Thursday morning was much like any other. The wages were on their way from the bank, the Wages Office was all prepared to split the money up into the small lots due in each wage packet. Security arrangements were perhaps a little tighter than usual because Soames had been worried by the fact that Stevens, once in the Trade Stores here, was now known to have taken part in a wages, snatch. Soames himself was at the gate house, waiting for the armoured van. From the moment it came through the gates with that money – nearly fifteen thousand pounds – it was his responsibility until the workers carried it off, that afternoon or the next morning, according to what shift they were on.

The van was due at a quarter past eleven today; the time of arrival always varied, to make sure that no one could check it too closely.

A small, plain van turned off the Great West Road towards the gatehouse, at five past eleven. It was close enough to the vital time for Soames to take special note of it. The driver wore a cap pulled low over his eyes, and that was enough to make Soames manoeuvre to get a closer look at him – the cap over the eyes was an old disguise. So Soames took a lot more time than usual checking the order which the driver had brought from a shop in Stepney. The driver had a moustache and he was fuller in the face than Stevens – but cheek-pads could make a fat face. He felt sure who this was, although he would not have recognised him had he not been on the look out.

He showed no sign of recognition or alarm.

"Okay," he said. "Take you half-an-hour to pick up that lot."

"'Bout that," said Stevens.

"Keep over to the right up at the loading bay," ordered Soames.

"Okay, guv'nor."

Soames let him drive up, and waited until the van was reversing into the loading bay before stepping inside the gatehouse. Another security man on duty saw the way his eyes were glistening, and asked eagerly:

"What's up, Bert?"

"Stop anything else that comes in—nd stop the money van," Soames said. "I won't be two jiffs." He picked up the telephone, dialled Whitehall 1212 and banged his clenched fist on a desk while he listened to the *brrr-brrrr*. Suddenly, a girl said: "Scotland Yard."

"Superintendent West—quick. For Mr Soames of Linstone's."

"Hold on, please," the girl said, and seemed to keep him waiting for a long time.

Roger was talking to Campbell, on one telephone, when his other phone rang just before ten past eleven that morning. He lifted the receiver of the second telephone without speaking into it, pressed it against his coat lapel, finished with Campbell, who was worrying about the Watford job, and then asked: "Who wants me?"

"There's a Mr Soames of Linstone's on the line."

Roger wondered: What does Soames want? He had no presentiment of an emergency, this was the last way he had expected the case to break.

"Put him through," he said.

"Mr West," said Soames, obviously fighting to keep his voice steady, "that man Stevens is here, in a plain van." Even before the sentence was uttered, Roger felt a rush of excitement, and Cope stared across. "He's up at the loading bay," Soames went on. "The money's due here in a few minutes."

"Keep that armoured van back until I get there," urged Roger. "I'll send plainclothes men from the Division and put a cordon round the factory. Don't start anything until I'm with you."

"I'll do what I can," said Soames. "That armoured van's on the way, though."

"Stop it, even if you have to hold it in a side street," ordered Roger. "I'll see you." He banged down the receiver and looked across at Cope. "We want a cordon round Linstone's on the Great West Road, quick. Stevens is there. Then we want road blocks on the Great West Road, ready to go into action if there's any need. Also fix guards at the railway siding behind Linstone's. Every possible way out has to be closed, and we've got twenty minutes."

"I'll fix it," Cope promised; already he had a telephone at his ear.

Over the counter in the Trade Stores, Stevens said:

"When's it due?"

"Between now and half past," Alec Gool whispered. He was making up the order for the plain van. "You got the t.g. all ready?"

"What do you take me for?"

"As soon as the van arrives, you go to the door." A man drew near. "How many wing mirrors is it?"

"Six. Trying to teach me my job?"

Alec said nothing, but went to get the wing mirrors.

"He's still inside the Trade Stores," Soames told Roger. Roger was outside the gatehouse, and the security chief of Linstone's was by the side of the car. "The wages van is pulled up in the Blundell Yard, that was the best I could do." The Blundell Tyre Company was next to Linstone's, and a six foot wall separated the grounds of the two factories.

"There's a cordon round the place," Roger said, "and road blocks ready to go into action at a moment's notice. Divisional chaps reported to you yet?"

"They're all ready."

"Have the cordon close in on the loading bay," Roger ordered. "Starting now."

"Right, Mr West."

Soames moved to the gatehouse, to telephone. Roger leaned back in his seat. His driver started the car, and drove slowly up the incline. The plain van was still in the loading bay but there was no sign of anyone near it, no sign that Stevens knew of any cause for alarm. Two detective inspectors were with Roger. They were opening the door as it drew to a standstill.

"Remember he's a killer," Roger said. "And remember he may have someone with him inside the warehouse. Dick, you come in with me."

"Right," a youthful detective said.

Roger got out of the car, and looked about. Plainclothes men were behind parked cars at corners, down on the drive between here and the gatehouse. He saw two lorries draw up, one each side of the Great West Road, each ready to swing across and block the way at a moment's notice. He did not think there was anything left undone. He moistened his lips, reminding himself that in here was Charley Blake's killer, the man who had stabbed with such vicious suddenness, a man of swift reactions and swift reflexes who was absolutely ruthless.

Roger pushed open the door of the warehouse, knowing that two other Yard men were at the far door. Dick followed him. There were three customers at the counter, including Stevens. Roger recognised Stevens at a glance; in front of the man was a tall pile of boxes and cartons, with the goods he was supposed to be collecting.

Roger went briskly up to him.

"I'm West of the Yard," he announced. "We won't have any trouble, Stevens. Just put up your hands—"

Stevens's right hand flashed to his pocket. Roger leapt at him. Dick rounded Roger and grabbed Stevens from the other side. The other customers hardly realised what was happening.

Roger saw something glisten in Stevens's hand, but it wasn't a knife – it was glass. *Tear gas.* Roger struck the man's hand aside, and the glass phial dropped to the floor, instead of bursting in his face and blinding him. Stevens, his face livid, tried to knee him in the groin, but Dick was already holding his other arm up in a hammer lock, and the surprise was complete. Stevens hadn't a chance.

Then a tear gas phial tossed from the other side of the counter broke against Roger's face. On the instant the gas stung his eyes, his nostrils and his mouth. His hold on Stevens slackened. He heard Dick cry out. He drove his clenched right fist into Stevens's defenceless stomach, and through the mists of gas and the tears as his eyes smarted, he saw the killer's face twist in agony.

"Get the doors and windows open!" Roger shouted. "And keep everybody inside." He had Stevens now, but there was still the man who had tossed the tear-gas phial from the other side of the counter, the last of the four Covent Garden killers.

Chapter Twenty

The Fourth Killer

There was one hope of getting out, Gool knew.

At the back of the trade warehouse was a cloakroom and lavatory, with an entrance from outside as well as from inside. He had studied it carefully, and had worked out what he would do if anything went wrong. Now, as the tear gas exploded into West's face, as Stevens struggled desperately, Gool moved away from the counter. One of the other warehousemen said:

"What's going on?"

"Got to get the security boys, quick," Gool said. "It's a hold-up."

"Gawd."

Gool pushed past, and rushed into the cloakroom.

"There's a wages hold-up," he announced breathlessly to two men inside. "Got to get the cops." He went out quickly, but did not hurry once he was outside. He saw two big men whom he knew were factory security men at the corner. "There's a hold-up," he shouted. "Wages snatch! In here." He held open the door and the two men came running. "I'll tell the gatehouse," he bellowed, as they went into the cloakroom.

Still not really hurrying, and wearing his brown smock, he walked down towards the gatehouse. Soames was now on his way up to the loading bay. Divisional police were moving up from the gatehouse, and it was now obvious that the raid had been anticipated, that the place was alive with plainclothes men.

"He told that Conway bitch and she's squealed," Gool said savagely to himself. Inwardly, he was seething with hatred and with frustration, he longed to hit out at someone, to make them suffer; but outwardly he was an ordinary, amiable youngster, looking rather excited and trying not to show it. "The bitch, wait till I get to her."

Between here and the Blundell Tyre Factory was the six foot wall, but there were gates in it, because there was considerable business between the two companies. Packers and warehousemen at the Trade Stores had keys, to get through; and Gool had one in his pocket.

He just had to keep his nerve.

He had to get to the ship and the woman who had betrayed them.

He hated her.

He went up to one of the Security men, actually one of the gatehouse keepers getting old for his job.

"There's some trouble up at the Trade Stores," he said to the old man. "Dunno what it is. I've got to get across to Blundell's for a couple of 5.45 by 15's." He showed an order which he had, made out on the Blundell Tyre Company. "Okay?"

The gatehouse telephone bell rang.

"Better wait a minute," said the Security man. "I'll see what this is." He went inside the little gatehouse.

Gool lit a cigarette, and stood looking up at the main building, where there was now a lot of activity. He saw men coming out, their hands at their eyes, one of them staggering as if he couldn't control his legs. Then he saw Steve Stevens, handcuffed to one of the detectives. He spoke to a plainclothes man near him:

"Looks as if they've got someone."

"They've got someone all right." The plainclothes man was watching the scene intently. "Where are you going?"

"Get some tyres, from next door. But I'm in no hurry – just right for a drag." He drew deeply at the cigarette. After a moment or two, the gatehouse keeper came out again. "No one's to leave the factory premises," he said. "Those tyres will have to wait."

"Suits me," said Gool. He leaned against the wall of the gatehouse, pulling steadily at the cigarette. The gatekeeper and the two plainclothes men didn't worry about him, he looked and sounded so innocuous. After a few minutes, he strolled round to the other side of the gatehouse, close to the wall with Blundell's. The gates were all closed and locked.

Gool walked up to the nearest, unlocked it, and stepped through calmly. Had he run, had he shown the slightest sign of being in a hurry, he would have been stopped. As it was, he went to the back of the factory, in full view of a lot of people, When he got to the back, he slipped off his brown smock; he was wearing a pullover underneath. He went to the big motor-cycle park, picked out a machine for which he had an ignition key, and drove openly down the drive of the tyre factory. At that gatehouse he thrust out a slip of paper, ostensibly a pass-out, and was hurtling into the Great West Road before the gatekeeper realised that he had been fooled.

The Blundell man had no idea what was happening at Linstone's. This was simply a breach of the regulations. He would find out who that young whipper-snapper was, and report him.

It was one o'clock.

Joyce sat in the little cabin, listening to someone talking on the radio, and knitting: knitting was the only way she had to pass the time. She had never known the hours drag so much as they had today. The crew had shore-leave, except a few on maintenance duty, but these seldom came up near the cabin, which Steve had arranged for her. It was usually the first mate's, she had been told. She kept looking at her watch and wondering if by chance Steve would be back any earlier than he had said. When she let herself think about it, and there was so much time for thinking, she knew that he was almost certainly committing some crime. She did not know for certain what he had done in the past, but everything pointed to the Covent Garden wages snatch – to cold blooded murder. She kept shutting out the vision of a man dying.

She heard a sound on the quayside, and jumped up.

Through the porthole, she saw a motor-cycle drawn up close to the ship. The front and the rider were hidden from her. Could Steve have come back on it? She turned towards the mirror fastened to the wall, her heart beginning to beat fast as it did whenever she believed that Steve was coming. In a queer way, since the realisation of trouble that had happened more often – there was a kind of sickening excitement which she had not known in the calmer days at the pub and at her home.

She put on powder and ran her comb through her hair. She heard footsteps in the gangway approaching the cabin, and for the first time she frowned; they weren't Steve's. Perhaps one of the ship's boys was coming to clean the cabin next door.

She heard the footsteps stop, and saw the latch of this door move; *was* it Steve? She turned with her back to the mirror as the door opened wide, and Alec Gool stepped in. Suddenly, awfully, she was in terror. He moved so swiftly, closing the door behind him. From the moment that he caught sight of her, he stared. He reminded her of Steve in those awful seconds at Brighton. His eyes seemed to be alight. He leaned against the door for a moment, and she saw how his breast heaved. "So he told you, and you squealed," he said. She drew a deep breath. "I—I don't know what you mean."

"You know," Alec said, thinly. "The police got him. They were ready for us. You must have tipped them off." "Steve? They can't have got Steve!" "They got him, and you know it. You stayed here in case he got away, so you would be waiting for him," Alec Gool said savagely. "They got him, and they saved the pay load we were going to snatch. He deserves what happened to him for telling you—"

"He didn't tell me! He—you're lying to me! The police haven't got him. They can't—"

"They've got him," said Alec. "But they're not going to get me. There's just one squealer who can name me to the cops—that's little Joyce Conway. *Dear* little Joycey. They're not going to take me. I'm leaving for a nice long voyage for my health. Before I go I'm going to do what Steve ought to have done at Brighton."

Alec put his hand into his pocket.

"No!" gasped Joyce. "No, I didn't tell anyone! I swear—"

Gool took his hand out of his pocket, and there was a click of sound. A blade stabbed out from the knife in his hand. It was a tiny cabin; he had only to take three strides to reach her.

"This is what you asked for," he said. "This is what you're going to get."

"*No!*" she screamed.

"It's okay—scream. The porthole's soundproof. No one is up this end of the ship. Go on, scream. I like to hear it. No one knows where I am, no one knows where you are, so it won't do you any good. Go on, scream."

He drew a step nearer.

She was sobbing.

"No, please, don't do it, don't do it! I didn't tell the police anything, I didn't know, I—"

He began to take another step forward.

As he did so, the door burst open behind him. He jumped, twisted round and lost his balance. He fell forward, making a wild, futile sweep towards Joyce with the knife, but he didn't touch her, and the knife blade stabbed into the bedding of the bunk. Three men crowded into the cabin, and one seemed to be on top of Alec Gool before he had stopped falling. Joyce heard a click. With terror still in her eyes, she saw that Alec was handcuffed to the man who had fallen on top of him.

She recognised one of the other men as Golloway, the divisional superintendent, who occasionally dropped in at the Hornpipe for a drink.

"All right, Mrs Conway," he said. "No need to be frightened now. Stevens told the Yard where we would find you, and we didn't waste any time. When we told Stevens Gool had got away he guessed what Gool would try to do, and made sure you couldn't come to any harm. Now take it easy—there's no hurry."

She was crying.

She kept on crying for a long time, from shock, from release from fear, and from a kind of grief.

On the following Monday, when all the excitement had died down, and the daily as well as the Sunday newspapers had used up as many headlines as the story would take, Roger waited for Calwin and his three sons. At precisely half past two, his telephone bell rang to announce their arrival. He went for them.

Calwin had dolled himself up in a navy-blue suit, and wore a comparatively subdued tie; his shoes shone as if lacquered. The sons, aged seventeen, fifteen and thirteen, looked as if their mother had scrubbed and polished them before this great occasion.

Calwin crushed Roger's hands, proudly introduced Bill, George and Ted, who all tried to out-crush their father, and then asked, booming:

"What'll happen to them crooks, Mr West? That's what I want to know. All four of them have been rounded up, one way or another, but will this pair *hang?*"

"They'll be convicted of capital murder, anyhow."

"How about this woman Stevens was living with?"

None of his sons even blinked.

"I doubt whether we shall be able to make a case against her," Roger said. "Stevens swears she knew nothing about it. It wouldn't surprise me if her worst crime was to be in love with the wrong man."

"Hey! Not going soft, are you?" demanded Calwin, and roared with laughter. "Now, how about the trip? I've promised my boys the Information Room, Records Office, Fingerprints—the lot. Hey?"

"And the lot it shall be," promised Roger.

He saw Joyce Conway later in the week, at the little terraced East End house. On the kitchen mantelpiece was a small photograph of Steve Stevens, in a metal frame, but that was the only sign that the man had been here so often. She was dressed in a nicely tailored two-piece suit, she looked pale, preoccupied and older, but not frightened.

"I came to tell you that the Public Prosecutor has decided to take no action against you," Roger said. "He accepts your statement that you had no knowledge of the crimes until that day at Brighton. And I'm sure you'll be glad to know that there won't be any need to call you as a witness, Mrs Conway."

She sat down heavily on an upright chair.

"Thank you," she said in a low-pitched voice. Obviously the possibility of being a witness had worried her most. "You're very good. Would you mind telling me how Steve is?"

"Very well," Roger said. "Would you like to see him?"

She closed her eyes.

"No," she said, after a pause. "No, I don't think that would do him any good—it wouldn't help either of us, not yet, anyhow. I'm very glad he's all right, though. He—he doesn't think I gave him away, does he?"

"He knows you didn't," said Roger. "Gool knows it, too. Have you decided what you're going to do?"

"I'm staying on at the Hornpipe," she answered. "Mr Harris has been ever so good. He says I can have my job back as soon as I want it. All my neighbours have been very good, too. Of course, they don't know that Steve spent so much time here as he did, but—"

"There's no reason why they should ever know," Roger said. He held out his hand. "If we can do anything to help at any time, Mrs Conway, let us know."

She held his hand, nodded, then watched him go; but she recovered enough to hurry to the front door to see him out.

He stepped into the narrow, ill-lit street, with its drab grey houses and the gas lamps and the slate roofs. He walked along to the corner, where he had left his car, watched by a dozen curious people at the windows of other little homes.

He was very thoughtful as he drove off. It had been a long case and a tricky one, and they had had their share of luck. They usually had. But they had solved it because he had stuck to it – because he had worked on it like a professional policeman.

Looking back over it, there were aspects which hardly seemed real.

Isobel Bennison, for instance—

Janet was going over to see her today, and together they were to visit the hospital. Bennison was not only out of danger, he would soon be able to get about. Old Revel had told him that his job was waiting for him. His disability would be no handicap in the work.

There were three ways to look at murder, Roger reflected. The way the police looked at it, the way those who suffered looked at it – and the killer's way. This particular killer had made a good woman love him deeply. Would anyone ever find out why he had become a killer?

JOHN CREASEY

GIDEON'S DAY

Gideon's day is a busy one. He balances family commitments with solving a series of seemingly unrelated crimes from which a plot nonetheless evolves and a mystery is solved.

One of the most senior officers within Scotland Yard, George Gideon's crime solving abilities are in the finest traditions of London's world famous police headquarters. His analytical brain and sense of fairness is respected by colleagues and villains alike.

'The finest of all Scotland Yard series' – New York Times.

GIDEON'S FIRE

Commander George Gideon of Scotland Yard has to deal successively with news of a mass murderer, a depraved maniac, and the deaths of a family in an arson attack on an old building south of the river. This leaves little time for the crisis developing at home ....

'Gideon of Scotland Yard emerges as one of the most real working detectives in modern fiction.... A sympathetic and believable professional policeman.' - New York Times

JOHN CREASEY

THE CREEPERS

"The prisoner's hand was thin and bony ... And in the centre of the palm was a pinkish mark. It was the shape of a wolf's head, mouth open, fangs showing. Although it was what he had expected to see, Inspector West felt a twinge of repugnance a stab not unrelated to fear. It was the fifth time he had seen the mark of the wolf – the mark of Lobo."

A gang of cat burglars led by Lobo cause mayhem as they terrorize the city. They must be stopped, but with little in the way of evidence the police are baffled. Just how can Inspector West manage to do this in what is a race against time before more victims succumb?

"Here is an excellent novel of law enforcement officers, harried, discouraged and desperately fatigued, moving inexorably ahead under the pressure of knowledge that they must succeed to save human lives." - Cleveland Plain-Dealer

"Furiously exciting" - Chicago Tribune

"The action is fast, continuous and exciting" - San Francisco News

John Creasey

The House of the Bears

Standing alone in the bleak Yorkshire Moors is Sir Rufus Marne's 'House of the Bears'. Dr. Palfrey is asked to journey there to examine an invalid - who has now disappeared. Moreover, Marne's daughter lies terribly injured after a fall from the minstrel's gallery which Dr. Palfrey discovers was no accident. He sets out to investigate and the results surprise even him . . . .

"'Palfrey' and his boys deserve to take their places among the immortals." - Western Mail

Introducing the Toff

Whilst returning home from a cricket match at his father's country home, the Honourable Richard Rollison - alias The Toff - comes across an accident which proves to be a mystery. As he delves deeper into the matter with his usual perseverance and thoroughness , murder and suspense form the backdrop to a fast moving and exciting adventure.

'The Toff has been promoted to a place of honour among amateur detectives.' – The Times Literary Supplement

21948201R00103

Printed in Great Britain
by Amazon